Headwater Holiday

HANNAH HOOD LUCERO

SKEETER HAWK LIBRARY PUBLISHING

This one is for you, Rosman...

For the years we spent together, for being the home I always miss and never tire of coming back to, and for the constant reminder of what real community and resilience looks like . . . TIGER STRONG!

In loving memory of Robert Lynn Morgan, Jayden Reynaldo, and Layne Jones.

Epigraph

As a little girl, I sailed your waters,
In a mighty green canoe.
I learned to swim, fish, and paddle,
On your shoals, it's where I grew.

My eyes have danced to your reflection,
As the sun mirrored off your skin.
From your banks, I've watched you glisten,
Sparking a light deep within.

As a woman, I have faced your weather,
I have watched you rise and fall.
Never did I fear a day
That you would take it all.

—Jessica Whitmire

Glossary of Terms

CAC—Common Access Card (Military ID)

EMP—Electromagnetic Pulse

EOD—Explosive Ordnance Disposal

HQ—Headquarters

HUMINT—Human Intelligence

IED—Improvised Explosive Device

NCO—Non-Commissioned Officer

OPSEC—Operations/Operational Security

OSINT—Open-Source Intelligence

PTSD—Post-Traumatic Stress Disorder

Chapter 1

Friday Evening, December 20th

BAH FREAKING HUMBUG!

All of her hard work, unprecedented achievements, and dress uniform littered with ribbons on the chest had led Rebecca Salazar to this place: Podunk, North Carolina.

Her first Christmas stateside in four years, and she was on the other side of the country from her parents. The two-stoplight town wasn't actually called Podunk, but what kind of name was Rosman? Every time she typed it into a text or email, autocorrect changed it to Roman. She'd much rather be in Rome instead of sitting on the side of the road with blue lights flashing behind her and festive Christmas lights blanketing the town up ahead.

She could practically smell the chestnuts and homemade gingerbread from a mile away, which might have been nice if she had time to stop and enjoy the delights of the season. Instead, she was living the beginning to a horrible cliché Christmas movie.

That might not be so bad either, if she were someone looking for Mr. Tall, Dark, and Handsome. He'd have crystal blue eyes and a British accent. Of course, he only came to this one-horse town to take care of his orphaned sister. A cop by day, he'd volunteer at the nursing home at night and deliver meals to shut-ins on Sundays. He'd donate his secret stash of inherited cash to the animal rescue shelter—because what would he need that fortune for when all that really mattered was a comfortable home and security for his sister . . . and his dream of falling in love with a strong-willed Latina.

Yeah, right. Keep dreaming, Salazar.

What was taking the cop so long, anyway? She sighed, having depleted her imaginative stores for the day. Reality was bleak.

Landlocked for the umpteenth time in her decade-long Navy career, she may as well be a caged animal. Recruiters who told naïve high school seniors of all the adventures of the open seas awaiting them should be forced to deploy to each and every forward operating base she'd been sent to. That would shut them up real quick. At the very least, someone could have warned her that picking a career in cyber intelligence and linguistics might end up costing her the promise of "seeing the world." Everywhere she'd been was nowhere anyone wanted to see, including this tiny corner of Appalachia.

The officer behind her finally exited the vehicle and meandered forward.

Hurry up, Barney Fife. Clock's ticking.

Icy snow crunched under the boots of the approaching hillbilly cop. Becky shivered against the chill blowing into the new-to-her Chevy pickup. The thing was obnoxiously red, which was likely why the cop pulled her over in the first place. Where was his Christmas spirit? Already in a dumpster somewhere with her own? Both of them would be working straight through the Lord's birthday without much cheer—especially if her intel was right.

"Evening, ma'am." He leaned over, smiling. Why did he look familiar? The scar along his right cheekbone grabbed her attention right off. His green eyes reminded her of the Grinch, too bright and alarmingly mischievous.

Hate, hate, hate. Double hate. Loathe entirely! She quoted the Grinch in her head.

His unruly blond locks and scruffy face were a disgrace to the uniform. Obviously these backwoods people didn't enforce any sort of standard for appearance, not that the man was out of shape or disheveled aside from the hair. He could at least have the decency to put a hat over that thick mop.

Becky raised an eyebrow and bit her tongue, shoving her fistful of credentials out the window. The officer furrowed his brow and stared at them for a beat before taking them.

"Uh . . . do you know why I pulled you over this evening?" He didn't bother looking through the registration and identification.

"I don't, but I'm certain it will make you downright joyful to enlighten me." Becky forced a half-smile. He smirked, and his stupid green eyes flashed with amusement. "Can you just write the ticket? I'm sort of in a hurry."

"That's interesting, because you weren't speeding at all. Going under the limit, actually." He raised both eyebrows. "Not from around here, huh?"

"Are you saying I don't look like a local? Is that an insult or a compliment?" She let too much snark slip into her tone. He only licked his lips, smile doubling in size. She couldn't hold her irritation in. "You're obviously profiling me."

"Right, right." His smile faded as his jaw flexed. "Because every white small-town cop is racist. Tell me, are you the pot or the kettle in this scenario? You're doing some profiling of your own right about now."

Okay, I earned that fair and square. At least he's not a pushover.

"Oh, please. I meant the red paint on the truck, Officer . . ." Becky attempted to read his name badge.

"*Deputy* Taylor. I'm sure there's a quip about Mayberry on the tip of your tongue—but you're a good four hours from there." He finally glanced at her ID, the smile returning.

Becky coughed to cover her snort. She'd picked the wrong character from the wholesome 1960s sitcom, and Deputy Taylor called her out as if he could hear every thought running through her head. To his credit, this guy was way better looking than Andy Griffith had ever been. If his first name turned out to be Andrew—which she had no intention of finding out—she'd pee her pants laughing.

Holding her military ID and papers back out toward her, he asked, "Has that ever worked for you, *Chief* Salazar?"

"What?"

"Throwing your common access card into the mix like every other veteran who passes through town." He rested his forearms on the open window and leveled a stare into her eyes, unnerving her. He knew the official name for a military ID, which meant he'd probably had one of his own. Becky cleared her throat and looked away, tossing the CAC on the passenger seat along with the registration and Colorado driver's license. She'd severely underestimated her audience. He leaned a little closer, smelling like a candy cane and asking, "Did you think I'd be impressed with your rank? Grateful enough for your service to let something slide? It's a common mistake. FYI, it rarely works with me. If anything, I'm more likely to throw the book at you."

Becky gulped, heat creeping up her neck. That's when she noticed the unmistakable tip of an arrow tattooed on his forearm. The uniform's long sleeve covered most of the ink, but she glimpsed enough of the Latin word *spiritus* to put two and two together.

Marine Special Operations Command. Of course. I should have recognized the swagger.

"I'm not trying to get out of anything." Gripping the steering wheel, she lifted her gaze back to his. "I asked you to write the ticket, didn't I? I'm only trying to be thorough."

He hummed and nodded. "I never intended to write you a ticket. Your driver's side taillight is out."

"Oh. And you don't ticket people for that? I-I should have paid more attention." Why did she suddenly feel the need to justify herself? "I actually bought the truck today."

"Even more reason to cut you some slack, right?" He waved at the driver of a blue Jeep as they slowly passed by. "Sometimes I write a warning. Then check up with folks to see if they rectify the situation."

"Right." She gestured to the town ahead of them. "You probably know most of the people around here."

"Welcome to Rosman, Chief. We've been expecting you." He pushed off the truck and gave a lazy salute. "And . . . *thank you* for your service."

"You too," she mumbled, causing him to halt his retreat.

"Excuse me?"

"The tattoo. You're a Raider?" Becky raised her eyebrows, waiting for his response.

"The tattoo." He nodded, then narrowed his eyes, looking almost disappointed. "You're observant. And so personable."

"Funny." Becky rolled her eyes.

She should have kept her mouth shut. Taylor took a step back toward her window, renewed curiosity etched on his face.

"Why exactly is a joint task force descending on my tiny town anyway? It's all very hush-hush."

She blinked at him, thrown off by his knowing about the task force. Small towns were the worst. The sheriff had been instructed to keep it to himself for the time being. Who else knew too much already? The last thing they needed was for people to panic. The plan was to stop the attack before anyone was the wiser.

"That's classified." She cleared her tightening throat.

"Of course it is." Deputy Taylor looked far from impressed. "Your top secret meeting is just up ahead on the right, best fajitas for three counties."

"Fajitas?"

"The Mexican restaurant." He nodded toward the glow of lights up ahead, which somehow seemed more classy and charming than they had ten minutes ago. "You can't miss it."

"Great." Becky put the truck in drive, strangely relieved that someone with combat experience might be readily at her disposal, equally irritated with how he clearly knew more than he was letting on. "I'll get the taillight fixed first thing tomorrow. Um, thanks."

"Yep." Taylor popped the *p* and walked away without another word.

Deputy Matthew Taylor settled into the warm seat of his cruiser, releasing the chuckle he'd been holding in. Rebecca Salazar—or *Stunner*, as she was affectionately referred to by the elite forces that worked with her—was more of a spitfire than he remembered. She clearly hadn't fixated on their one encounter like he had for the last six years. He couldn't blame her. The single meeting had been brief, and he was only one of a dozen Raiders in the room with her that day. Half of those operators hit on her harder than he had. Though she'd seemed grateful that he at least plied her with hot coffee when he took his shot.

Word on the convoy was that she'd had flawless instincts from the very start of her career, which was how she'd risen through the ranks so quickly. No Ranger, SEAL, Raider, or "other guys" who'd ever worked off her intel would question the merit of her reputation. Her monitoring of terrorist OSINT—Open-Source Intelligence—had led to the capture or killing of hundreds of high-threat targets. The kicker was that everybody with an internet connection had access to the junk those idiots posted from caves and compounds, but Salazar had figured out how to filter through the garbage and find the treasure troves that allowed guys like him to neutralize major threats. Sheriff Woodhouse hadn't mentioned that *she* was the one coming to town with alarming news, only that a Navy chief was heading up the task force.

This is more serious than I thought, unless she's completely shifted gears from what she used to do.

He pulled out behind Salazar as she made her way to the only Mexican restaurant in town. The sheriff wasn't a proud man and had quickly realized that Matt's prior experience made him the right person to put on the task force in his place. What would Salazar think when he followed her into the parking lot and then the restaurant? At first, being the assigned liaison from the sheriff's department had irritated him. But now? His curiosity and the anticipation of endless opportunities to push Salazar's buttons had him smiling ear to ear despite the foreboding thoughts of what her presence here might mean. Skills like hers were reserved for the front line. Rumor was, she'd put boots on the ground in more than one mission, because her HUMINT—Human Intelligence—collection was even more impressive than the online stuff. "A walking Rosetta Stone," someone had called her.

One thing was for sure—she wasn't the least bit shy. He laughed again, imagining what sassy thing she might pop off with next.

Pulling up to the Acapulco restaurant, Matt threw the cruiser into park and killed the engine. He watched as Salazar gathered a box from the passenger floorboard of her truck and struggled under the weight for a moment before she found her bearings. The woman was taller than he remembered—probably a good five feet eight inches—but otherwise looked the part of her Hispanic surname. Her dark brown hair was in a tight, low bun despite her being in civilian clothes. The slacks and button-up blouse were what one might expect for a Navy NCO on assignment to a small town in the middle of nowhere, Not too flashy, but not casual either.

Matt glanced around the parking lot. His pulse ticked up at the five government vehicles in the front. How many more were on the other side of the building? If this was so top secret, why were they meeting at a public restaurant? Why not at the high school auditorium or the basement of a local church?

Salazar seemed to take a deep breath, still not walking. Was she *glaring* at the ground? She took a tentative step and stopped, her foot slipping slightly. Matt took pity on her, realizing that the ground was slick with yesterday's snow, which had slightly melted during the day and refrozen into a thick sheet of ice as the sun got lower in the sky. He jumped out of his cruiser and strode toward the woman, planning to unburden her.

"Ugh." She glanced up at him. "What now?"

Maybe he should keep walking and let her struggle.

"Can I take that off your hands?" He nodded toward the box. Her brow furrowed for a moment before a sheepish, defeated expression filled her face.

"Would you mind?"

"Not at all." He stepped forward and reached for the box. The single step Salazar took toward him nearly ended in disaster. In a moment as quick as lightning, her foot slipped again. The box slammed into Matt's chest, nearly knocking him down. Thankfully, he was able to grab both the box and Salazar's arm, stopping her from cracking her head on the ice-covered gravel.

"Sorry." She grimaced, righting herself. "And thanks. Again."

"Sure." He looked down at her feet. "Those shoes are a hazard."

"No kidding." She huffed, turning back toward the truck and carefully slide-stepping to it. Jerking the door open, she climbed into the passenger seat and reached into the floorboard. Pulling a pair of socks out of black combat boots, she grinned up at him. "I hate heels anyway."

Matt snickered at the combo of her boots and slacks when she hopped back to the ground and slammed the truck door.

"I can take that now." She held her arms out for the box.

"I've got it." He nodded toward the restaurant. "They'll be sending out a search party soon. We're late."

"We?" Salazar groaned. "You're not supposed to know about this."

"The sheriff handed me the reins. He didn't give me many details, but he said he doesn't have the experience you're gonna need." Matt started walking, falling into step beside Salazar as she released a sigh and seemed to accept the situation for what it was. "What's this about?"

"You'll hear with the rest of them. But I don't know how I'm supposed to talk about this in such a public space." She wrinkled her nose. "No one seems to be worried about OPSEC, do they? That's a problem."

"I was thinking the same thing. One would think, as cryptic as everyone has been so far, that operational security would be at the top of the list." Matt waited for Salazar to get the door. "Maybe they think the staff won't understand any of it—you know, if they're *profiling* folks."

"You're not going to let me forget that one." Salazar rolled her eyes, but he caught the slight smile on her lips before she turned away, opening the door to the sound of a crowd enjoying mariachi Christmas music. The savory aroma of sizzling hot onions and peppers made his mouth water and reminded him just how long it had been since lunch.

When they entered the restaurant, Sheriff John Woodhouse jumped up from his seat on the far wall, waving them both over.

"Taylor," the sheriff called. "You're late."

"Sorry, boss." Matt shot a wink at Salazar. "Got held up by the chief here."

"I'm pretty sure it was you and the flashing lights that made *me* late," Salazar countered, then stretched out her hand when they reached the table. "Sheriff Woodhouse."

"Chief Salazar, call me John." He gestured to the empty booth across from him. "Please sit. Sorry I didn't wait to order. I wasn't sure you'd make it before closing."

"No worries. If we're being informal, you can call me Becky." She slid all the way into the booth, pursing her lips when Matt placed the box on the floor and sat right next to her. Clearing her throat, she asked, "When am I supposed to brief the room, John?"

"You haven't heard." The sheriff smiled uncomfortably across the table. "Not tonight, I'm afraid. We have a briefing set for nine in the morning at Town Hall. Seems the FBI is holding us up—big shocker."

"No. That's unacceptable." Becky—not the nickname Matt would have pegged Chief Petty Officer Rebecca Salazar with—tensed in the booth. "There isn't time to waste."

"I'm sorry, Becky." John shrugged, looking helpless about it all. "It's really out of my hands. I honestly thought this was your rodeo, but a Special Agent Simms moved the times around and sent out a mass email. You should have gotten it."

Becky flinched at the name of the FBI agent, her hands balling into fists as John relayed the message.

"Of course he'd do something so asinine. I was buying a truck. And then I was driving the truck," Becky grumbled, fishing her phone from her pants pocket and tapping away at it until she found what she was looking for. She seemed to hold her breath for a beat. Slamming the phone down on the table, she muttered, "That *jerk*. I'll kill him."

"What's that?" John paused with his fork in the air, setting it down cautiously on his plate.

Becky forced a smile and shook her head as if attempting to let the situation roll off of her tense shoulders—which didn't look like it was working. "What are we doing here if there isn't any official business being conducted?"

"Eating. Figured that was obvious." John kicked Matt lightly under the table. "You need to get acquainted with the names and faces in this room, Taylor. Understand?"

"Yes sir." Matt sighed, glancing at the tables surrounding them. There wasn't a familiar face among the crowd, but he recognized the type. Bureaucrats and brass, the lot of them. He leaned toward Becky, saying, "Your friends are even more *commanding* than you are."

"I don't know any of these people." She scoffed. "I didn't get a say in who each agency sent, trust me."

Matt looked around again. "Is anyone in here not a general or a spook?"

"Sure." Becky sat back with a sigh. "There's the three of us."

Before Matt could ask exactly which agencies were represented, his favorite waiter came to the table, slapping him on the shoulder and asking when they would go fishing for trout again. He dusted off his Spanish skills and told Oscar to name the date. When he'd ordered his dinner, Oscar turned to Becky expectantly. She hesitated, surprise etched on her face as she ordered the same thing as Matt. Oscar beamed at her when she spoke Spanish that sounded a lot closer to his than Matt's version.

"*Gracias,* Oscar." John's thick Appalachian accent made the words almost comical.

Their waiter bustled off and Becky crossed her arms, turning in the booth so she faced Matt. "You speak *nearly* perfect Spanish."

"My stepmom is from Guatemala. She started teaching me at six years old." He answered her unasked question. "In fact, she and Dad are gone to visit her family for *Navidad.*"

"Good. That's good." Becky nodded, eyes glazing over like her mind was somewhere else entirely.

In an attempt to draw her back, he said, "Your accent sounds like Oscar's. Is your family from El Salvador?"

Becky's lips pressed into a thin line. "My family is from Denver."

"You know what I mean." Matt glowered at her, mind fixating on the piece of information he'd gleaned. Her Colorado ID was his first clue, but her confirmation of being from Denver had his smart mouth running away from him. "You're from Colorado and don't know how to walk on icy ground?"

"I've been gone a long time," she retorted. "And I was matching Oscar's dialect. That's sort of my thing."

"Right. Your linguist thing." Matt poked her shoulder, garnering a glare. "You speak like five languages, right?"

"Something like that. You sure seem to know a lot about me, and here I don't know much of anything about you." She cocked her head to the side, clearly annoyed at her lack of intel.

"I bet you hate that, don't you, *Stunner*?"

"You really have done your research. No doubt asked some of your old buddies if I earned my insignia with merit or by way of diversity, equity, and inclusion." She said the final three words like they were something that might get stuck to the bottom of her boots.

Matt couldn't help the laugh that rose from his chest but didn't give her the satisfaction of confirming or denying her theory.

"What was your rank, Marine?" Her voice took on a rigid authority that nearly made him laugh again. Was she actually trying to pull rank? He had her right where he wanted her.

"Isn't that in your classified files?" He'd poke this bear to her breaking point if she let him. "Doesn't really factor in at this point, does it? I'm just Deputy Taylor these days."

"Whatever. Be cryptic. I'll figure it out on my own." She huffed. "My grandparents came from Costa Rica, to answer your earlier question."

"Beautiful country." Matt nodded. "Great people. Usually so nice . . ."

"I see the two of you have already hit it off." John looked between them, raising an eyebrow.

"Oh, yeah." Matt smiled at John. "Practically besties."

The sheriff let out a hearty laugh and picked up his fork, shaking his head. When he'd swallowed a bite of his rice, he pointed the fork at Matt but addressed the chief.

"He's a pain in my butt, Becky."

"No." She feigned shock. "I can't imagine that."

"But he's the best deputy I've ever had. Hard worker, low maintenance, and way too skilled for his own good." John sang Matt's praises, making him squirm in the booth. "He talks too much when he's bored or excited. But you can trust him to get the job done, whatever it is. That's why I looped him in. Trust me, he's the asset you want."

"That . . ." Her eyes darted to Matt for a split second. "Actually, that makes a lot of sense. I've worked with guys like him before."

Matt covered his mouth with his hand, swallowing a chuckle. She *really* didn't remember him at all. It might have injured his ego if he wasn't looking forward to rubbing it in her face later.

"Oh, I don't know about that." John shook his head. "He's one of a kind."

"Yeah. A real special sort." Becky pursed her lips. "No doubt he'll come out the hero in the end."

"I can hear you guys." Matt waved his hand between them, but they both ignored him.

"You can take that to the bank." John winked at Becky. "He'll get this wrapped up in a day."

"I hope you're right, John." The deflated way Becky said the words without a hint of sarcasm made the hair on Matt's arms rise.

A familiar energy surged through his chest. Suddenly his sleepy little town seemed as foreign as the countries he'd deployed to in the Marines. The morning couldn't come soon enough. It was all he could do not to rip the lid off of Becky's box of intel and satisfy his rabid curiosity.

Oscar's reappearance with their food barely registered in his mind. Was he seriously about to reenter the world of counterterrorism? He didn't doubt his ability to step back into that role, but the idea that it was hitting this close to home had him wishing he'd ordered a lighter meal than the massive sizzling plate of fajitas in front of him.

Chapter 2

EARLY SATURDAY MORNING, DECEMBER 21ST

BECKY RAN A BRUSH through her dripping wet hair, building and rebuilding her mental to-do list for the day. She'd hoped to get the briefing behind her and jump straight into action this morning, but—per usual—bureaucrats were dragging their feet.

Maybe they didn't believe her intel. She could hardly believe it herself. Four days ago, Army Rangers had stumbled across small bits of a plan to attack a tiny corner of western North Carolina. The plans were in an *al-Qaeda* stronghold in Yemen, of all places. Fire had destroyed almost everything in the compound, but at least they'd saved enough to know about Rosman.

After pushing her team around the clock to find anything possibly related to the pending attack, she'd had seven of the best analysts that she knew comb through every spec of data and intel, and each one of them came to the same conclusion. Something sinister was going down on Christmas Day, and it would originate in or near the smaller of the two incorporated places in Transylvania County, North Carolina. Not large enough to be a city, Rosman was a *town*. Population: 754.

Rustling outside of the secluded cabin she'd rented made Becky freeze with her brush in her hair. It was probably local wildlife. She listened for three long beats before another noise made her suck in a breath. It sounded like the tailgate on her truck had been let down.

Slowly placing the brush in the sink, she crept out of the bathroom, grabbing her Glock 19 from the holster she'd hung up behind the bedroom door. Luckily, she hadn't turned any other lights on and probably wouldn't be seen slinking across the kitchen to the window. It was still somewhat dark outside, making her grit her teeth in frustration.

Her blood ran cold when she spotted a flashlight at the rear of her truck. She ducked to the floor, stilling her nerves and preparing to react in a manner that wouldn't get her killed. She could go straight back to the bathroom, lock herself in, and call the sheriff, but whoever was out there could be long gone before help arrived. If the perp thought they could rig her truck with an IED or cut the brakes and get away unscathed, they had another thing coming.

Without another second of hesitation, Becky headed for the back door on the side of the cabin opposite the truck. It wasn't ideal, being alarmingly close to a steep drop-off, but she would have to manage. The cold air nearly knocked her back into the cabin, and instantly she regretted rushing out with bare feet, spaghetti straps, and a still-soaked head of hair. If someone got the jump on her, she'd die of exposure, assuming they didn't finish her off right on the spot.

The deck board nearest the steps creaked when she put her weight on it. She paused, slowly lifting her foot back up and attempting the step beyond it. A silent breath of relief sent a stream of white out in front of her. The rest of the steps proved to be as solid and quiet, and she pressed herself against the cabin to keep a safe distance from the drop-off a few feet away. Her heart was beating so erratically in her chest, it sent a pounding into her head.

By the time she made it around to the front edge of the cabin, there was enough light in the sky that the culprit no longer needed his flashlight. He seemed to be finishing his work, quietly lifting the tailgate and relatching it.

"Don't move." She projected her voice, staying far enough away that she could duck and run if need be.

"Don't shoot," a familiar voice responded.

"Taylor?" A minimal amount of relief trickled into her chest, even though she couldn't see his face. Slowly turning with his hands in the air, the deputy faced her. "What the heck are you doing here, messing with my truck?"

"I fixed the taillight. Could you maybe lower that?" He pointed at the gun in her hands. "Please."

She inhaled a deep breath and pointed the Glock at the ground, still on edge. "Why?"

"Because taking a bullet isn't how I prefer to start my Saturdays."

Becky glared at the obnoxious man. "I mean why did you fix the taillight? I told you I'd take care of it."

She could just make out the lift of his eyebrows and how he fought off a smile. "The auto parts store doesn't open until ten this morning. I assume we'll both be knee-deep in the action by then, and I had a feeling you wouldn't want to slow down the momentum for something so trivial."

"You happened to have a bulb for my exact make and model . . . lying around?"

"Noooo." He dragged the word out, lowering his hands. "My cousin owns the parts store I mentioned. He came back after closing last night so I could grab it for you."

"Wow. That's—" Becky cleared her throat, shivering now that her adrenaline was tapering off. Her tank top offered zero warmth, but at least her flannel-covered legs weren't as icy as her bare arms. "That's really thoughtful of you, Taylor. What do I owe you?"

"Call me Matt, and I'll call us even." His eyes swept over her before he diverted them back to the tailgate. "You should get dressed. You'll catch your death out here."

"I'm fine," she lied, refusing to shiver again or flinch at all. The idea that "Matt" might experience any measure of satisfaction from ingratiating himself with good deeds and sound advice had her mouth popping off before she could think it through. "We're even when I say we're even. You drink coffee?"

His narrowed side-eye screamed, "Obviously."

"You're in charge of brewing, Devil Dog. Come on." She turned for the stairs, leading him around the deck to the door she'd left cracked open. Flipping on the light, she pointed toward the kitchen. "Use the Screaming Peach breakfast blend I left on the counter. I don't know what is in that yellow mystery can or how long it's been here, but it smells like a skunk died . . . in a vat of fermented mare's milk."

"Hey, I like kumis."

Becky stopped in the doorway to her room. "Me too, just not with dead skunk in it."

Matt laughed and disappeared into the kitchen as Becky shut herself in the room. Taking a deep breath, she leaned against the door. Her hands shook, causing a small rattle to come from the Glock she still held. She pushed off the door and holstered the firearm, then went to work readying herself. By the time she had her hair, makeup, and clothes perfectly in place, the smell of not only coffee but also bacon made her stomach growl.

"What is he doing now?" she said to herself, turning the bathroom light off and grabbing her plain black coat on the way out of the bedroom.

"Hey, I saw the bacon and eggs in the fridge—I was curious—and thought I'd whip up some breakfast for you."

"For me? You're not going to eat?"

"Already ate at my place. It's not far from here, if you find yourself in need of some *sugar* while you're in town."

"Is that an innuendo?" She narrowed her eyes. "I know what 'sugar' means in the south."

"Why, Chief. I'm shocked." He didn't look the least bit shocked. "I meant for you to borrow baking necessities, of course. I'm not sure it's appropriate to discuss kissing at this point. Why don't we start with coffee and conversation and see how things develop? It's not out of the question."

"Good grief," she mumbled to herself, cheeks burning. To Matt, she said, "Could we not?"

"I'll let the idea marinate." He extinguished the burner under the skillet and turned to get a plate from the cabinet nearest the sink. How did he know where everything was? What a creeper.

"You're one of those relentless neighborly types, aren't you?" She plopped down into one of the chairs at the small round table just beyond the kitchen, hanging her jacket on the back of it.

"And you're one of those sullen feminist types?" He threw a snarky smile over his shoulder.

"No," she said firmly. "I'm—"

Matt paused midway through plating her breakfast, looking at her until she continued.

"I like to keep things professional."

"Oh, yeah. I can totally see that." Sarcasm dripped from his words. "Flirting with cops to get out of tickets. Literally throwing yourself at good Samaritans when they only want to carry a box for you. Inviting coworkers in for coffee and suggesting an exchange of 'sugar.'" He put the small skillet into the sink and added air quotes around the last word.

Becky's mouth fell open. Not only was most of what he said blatantly false, his insinuations were so far beyond inappropriate, she was at a loss for words.

Matt sauntered over, placing the plate of food in front of her. He had the gall to lift his calloused finger to her chin and apply light pressure until she closed her mouth. Again, the scar on his cheek caught her eye. It was so distinctly familiar, like she had fixated on one just like in the past, and for some reason, raw emotions were associated with the flaw. His face reminded her of fear and loss but somehow simultaneously brought her comfort.

"I'm joking, Becky." He leaned close, lowering his voice to whisper. "Clearly."

As quickly as he'd invaded her space, he turned back to the kitchen, walking toward two coffee mugs on the counter.

"Clearly," she repeated, stunned and unsure as to why she had butterflies in her stomach. Something was so *off* about this guy, but not in a way that truly alarmed her. His antics were familiar. The stereotypical special forces operator, sure of himself and determined to make her take the bait. She'd never fallen for it before, and she wasn't about to start today. "I shouldn't have invited you in. I wasn't thinking. I, uh, don't suppose you'll keep this whole thing to yourself?"

"And now you want me to *lie* about us sneaking around?" He bit his lip, sitting down across from her with both coffees. He had an annoying glint in his Grinchy eyes as he pushed her mug across the smooth, dark wood of the table. "You like it black, right? Like a trusty M4 carbine."

"Y-yeah." A strange sense of déjà vu crept over her.

"Yeah? So what is our cover story for this thing between us?" He grinned as if she'd confirmed his first question and not his second.

"I *mean*, I take my coffee black," she snapped. "And there's no sneaking around. Nothing at all between us. Stop putting words in my mouth."

"You're the one who called this a thing." He just wouldn't shut up.

"Fine. Tell whoever you want. I'll simply deny, deny, deny."

"Nah. It's our little secret. So much more fun that way." The humor left his face as he studied his coffee and took a deep breath. "How bad is it? Whatever is going down."

"It's . . . I'm not sure." She took a bite of the bacon, which was perfectly crisp. The eggs looked equally delicious, and the coffee smelled like heaven in a cup. No way was she boosting Matt's already inflated ego by telling him any of that though. "Thanks—for the taillight and for making all this. You didn't need to go out of your way for me."

Her thanks seemed to fall on deaf ears. "I can't take it, Becky. Break protocol for a second. Please tell me what's going on."

"Okay. And then we're even . . . for all this *hospitality*."

"Fair enough." He nodded once.

"There's an attack planned for Christmas Day. An EMP is possible." She glanced at her phone, trying to remember if she'd backed everything up to the cloud. An electromagnetic pulse was the stuff of nightmares for someone who depended on technology as heavily as she did.

"No IEDs, right?" Matt interrupted her panicked thoughts.

"Improvised explosives are highly probable, actually." Becky gulped, watching Matt's face for signs of the PTSD many veterans dealt with on a daily basis. He didn't flinch at the news, which was reassuring. "I pray to God there's nothing worse than that."

The pressure in her brain had been building for four long days. Speaking the words aloud to Matt released some of that pent-up anxiety. He would grasp what it all meant, probably more than the FBI, Homeland, and myriad of other agency representatives she'd repeat it to later.

"This doesn't make sense." Matt sat back in the chair. "There are way better targets. What's the point of hitting this area with weapons like that?"

"I dunno." Becky picked up her coffee, taking a sip and nearly getting distracted by the rich flavor. She'd brewed this same brand a thousand times. Why did it taste so much better today? Maybe being destined to fall for Deputy Taylor wasn't the worst thing in the world. If he made her coffee every day, she might just change her tune about flirting with disaster. "A dozen people way smarter than me have analyzed it from every angle."

"I doubt there are a dozen people smarter than you." Laugh lines appeared around his eyes as he leaned forward to rest his forearms on the table.

"*Anyway.*" She sighed in exasperation. "I can't make heads or tails of the why, but there's no denying that they'll be using some familiar tactics, and this is the target area."

"Western North Carolina in general?" He took another sip from his mug, eyeing her over the rim.

"*Rosman,* North Carolina. Specifically. Or at least this part of the county. Though there are vague references to the whole state being affected . . . and Tennessee." She took another bite of breakfast, chewing on her thoughts at the same time. "You're from Rosman, right?"

Matt nodded. "Born and raised."

"Does a railroad run near here?"

"Nothing operational." He shook his head.

"Talk to me about natural resources."

"Trees, a few minerals maybe—potential lithium mines? Apples and trout." He shrugged. "It's nothing that will destabilize anything major . . . unless there's something I don't know about. That's possible, by the way."

"Is that an ounce of humility I'm detecting?" She hummed, poking eggs with her fork. "I wasn't expecting that."

"I'm full of surprises." He winked.

"Sure you are. Back to the facts. Everything you said lines up with the little research I was able to do on the plane. I was hoping I'd missed something obvious." She waved it off. "Surely with all the heads we're putting together, we'll figure it out and stop whatever's coming. I wish we had more time, but I've seen worse plans thwarted in way less. We've got this."

"Definitely." He didn't sound convinced.

A knock at the front door made both of them stand up too quickly, as if they'd been caught stealing candy from a convenience store. They nearly butted heads, and Becky lost her footing. For the second time in less than twelve hours, Matt stopped her from biffing it hard. She sucked in a breath, annoyed that his hands on her shoulders felt more intriguing than irritating.

"You're so accident-prone." His teasing tone was back, irking her—or so she insisted to herself.

"I'm not usually." She stepped back, slapping his hovering hands away. "You're probably to blame."

"Wouldn't that be something?" A satisfied smile spread across his face, and she got the sudden urge to slap it off.

A second knock reminded her why they'd jumped to their feet in the first place. She stomped toward the door, hesitating when she saw the FBI badge hanging around the neck of a man whose face was hidden from view but whose posture was unmistakably familiar. Sending up a silent prayer that just this once, she was wrong, Becky opened the door. The answer to her prayer was a swift and resounding "Nope."

Could this whole thing get any worse?

"Hey, Becks." The smooth bravado of her ex-fiancé grated her already frazzled nerves. The pet name she used to love made her nauseous.

"Don't call me that," she snapped.

He stepped inside without an invitation, ignoring her and saying, "Coffee smells good."

"Come on in, *Bobby*." She shut the door with a flourish. Childish satisfaction coursed through her when she heard the irritated clearing of his throat. Nothing got under his skin more than his father's nickname for him.

Rob stopped in his tracks, having spotted Matt. "You have company."

Becky groaned internally. Rob didn't need this kind of ammunition in his arsenal. He'd use it. "Special Agent Robert Simms, meet Deputy Matthew Taylor . . . and so on."

Becky sat back down and dug into her eggs, refusing to look at either of them. This entire morning would humiliate her into an early grave.

"You're the former Marine that Sheriff Woodhouse mentioned." Rob stuck his hand out to Matt.

Becky cringed. Robert Simms was such a jerk. He knew good and well there was no such thing as a "former" Marine. He had some sort of complex about military guys and went out of his way to land lightly veiled insults to their faces and openly mock them behind their backs. He'd accused her more than once of having unsavory relations with guys on deployments. Of course it was all in his head and likely because of his own guilty conscience.

She tuned out the conversation happening beside her, gripping her fork so hard, a pain shot up her arm. Why would Rob think he was at all welcome here? It was more inappropriate than Matt showing up. It had been Rob's affair with a younger agent in his field office that put an abrupt end to their engagement only days before the wedding. Thankfully, Becky had listened to the voice in her head that told her something was off. If she hadn't dug into Rob's communications like he was one of the jihadists she hunted at work, she would have made the biggest mistake of her life.

Three years later, Becky was still a bit bitter about the botched attempt at a relationship. The least Rob could have done was ask to *not* be assigned to her task force. No, the least he could have done would have been to show up on time and not put more pressure on everyone by delaying the mission.

Pompous jerk.

Sure, she'd seen his name on the list and all his narcissistic replies to group emails, but she'd convinced herself that shame would keep him from actually showing his face here. He could have had a family emergency, caught a bad case of monkeypox, or driven off a cliff—allowing *anyone* else to come in his place. Of course that had been false hope, and in the back of her mind, she knew it. Rob didn't have the moral capacity to feel shame, nor would he pass up the opportunity to take credit for stopping jihadists from terrorizing small-town America.

"What are you doing here?" Becky blurted out, dropping the fork on the table. Curse Rob for ruining her appetite when Matt's cooking was delicious. By the looks on the men's faces, she'd interrupted their conversation at a pivotal moment. She couldn't care less.

Rob looked to the floor before dragging his poop-brown eyes back up to hers—appropriate, since he was full of it. Did he really think she'd buy the humble act?

"I wanted to make sure we're . . . good." He blinked a few times and pursed his lips.

"No, Rob. We are not 'good.'" She stood up, glaring and poking him in the chest. "It's bad enough that you're here at all, but you slowed down my op, and that could cost countless lives. Don't you dare send out another email on that thread unless it has useful information. *Information*, Robert. Not instructions. So help me, I'll destroy you if you get in my way again."

She glanced at Matt, who took a step back and raised his blond eyebrows toward his too-long wavy hair. The visual differences of the men, Matt with his fair features and Rob with hair darker than her own, were a stark contrast. A lightning-fast flash of old westerns she'd watched with Dad ran through Becky's mind like a reel. Matt was the white hat local hero—not at all how she'd wanted to view him five minutes ago—and Rob was the city slicker, rolling into town to upend life on the ranch.

"Becks." Rob reached his hand out toward her, making her recoil all the way back into the chair at the table. "Come on."

"Get out," she seethed through gritted teeth. "And I told you—don't call me that. Last warning."

"Okay." He raised both hands in the air. "I'll see you both at the briefing."

"If you had any decency at all, you'd head straight back to D.C. and send someone else. Someone qualified," she called over her shoulder, flinching when he slammed the door.

Chapter 3

MATT SAT BACK DOWN at the table, slightly shaken by "Rob" popping up out of nowhere and what he assumed was an uncharacteristic outburst from Becky. She kept her cool when she thought there was some sort of ax murderer outside her cabin, then the FBI jerk waltzed in and suddenly she turned into a basket case. Their past must be riddled with something uglier than Matt's cousin's mangy mutt, Bocephus.

"I'm guessing I don't have to worry about a love triangle with Rob." Matt broke the uncomfortable silence that had fallen in the agent's wake.

"Don't start." Becky stood, taking her half-full plate to the sink and staring out the kitchen window. Her shoulders were more tensed up than a copperhead ready to strike, giving Matt the sense that he should tread lightly for the rest of the morning. Finally she asked, "Where did you park, anyway?"

"Bottom of the hill." He gestured in that general direction, though she wasn't looking at him. "I didn't want to wake you."

"You have boundary issues." Her accusation wasn't entirely off base, but the tone seemed to be meant for Rob.

"I've been told as much before." He bit down on the inside of his cheek. Nothing about the current situation was funny. Smiling about it might elicit another tantrum.

"Rob is my ex, if that wasn't painfully obvious."

"Ex-husband?" Matt tried to keep his face from revealing his disgust. He couldn't picture Becky married to a guy who seemed to put more effort into his hair than his job.

"Thankfully not. It was a close call though."

"I'm guessing he's at fault for the breakup." Matt made his voice light, not wanting to add any more weight to her now-slumped shoulders.

"Depends who you ask." She turned back around. "Rob would tell you I was emotionally unavailable and too focused on my career."

"So he cheated."

"Hmmm." A bitter, throaty laugh mixed with her hum. "You're smarter than you look."

"And you're surly toward me, not because I'm a man . . . but because Rob is the worst sort. So you're not a feminist but definitely a man-hater. That's too bad for us good guys, ya know?"

Becky shook her head, a smile pulling at her lips.

"You're seriously brazen, Matt—it's to be expected, I know. Rangers, Raiders . . . all of you operators are notorious flirts." She sighed, adding, "You've got some sort of high-stakes romance already planned out in your head, don't you?"

"Of course. Don't you?" he countered. "We're on the clock. We've got what—four or five days to solidify this 'thing'?" He ignored the narrowing of her eyes and plowed ahead. "Look how far we've already come."

"I'm listening."

"A small-town deputy pulls over the out-of-towner for a perfect meet-cute, check." He mimed a checkmark in the air.

"Perfect?" She tried to interject, but he ignored her interruption.

"Forced proximity—the booth at Acapulco last night, cabin this morning, and the task force—check."

"You trapped me in that booth. And you–you tricked me into inviting you inside." She pointed an accusatory finger at him, taking a step toward where he sat. "No one forced you to come here. And how are you so well-versed in romance tropes?"

"I did not trick you. My plan was to act as the taillight fairy and let you wonder how the thing magically fixed itself." He shook his head slowly and ignored her question. No way was he admitting to his secret obsession with romantic comedies. "How dare you?"

"How dare me?" She widened her eyes, jabbing both thumbs into her own chest.

"You pointed a gun at me." He stood, taking a step forward and placing his hands on his hips.

"I thought you were cutting my brakes or strapping a bomb to my undercarriage!" She took another step closer to him, her face turning red with anger or embarrassment, he wasn't sure which.

Matt snorted. The visual of a coiled copperhead flooded into his mind again, but he stomped ahead anyway. "You said undercarriage."

"You're a child."

"I cooked you breakfast." He chewed on his lip, enjoying himself too much.

"You—That was really tasty, actually." She blinked, seeming to lose her next point.

"So you wasted it because . . .?"

"Stupid Rob," she seethed, back on track. "Everything bad is because of him."

"Right." He nodded once, firmly agreeing. "Stupid Rob."

Somehow they'd gotten closer than Matt realized. Becky's face smoothed out, and a smile tugged at the right corner of her mouth.

"Is this when we let the angst get the better of us?" he whispered, glancing at her lips.

She gulped, eyes going wide. "You–you're going to have to try a lot harder than—No!" She shook her head. "The answer is a flat no."

He crossed his arms and heaved a dramatic sigh. "You need to take an improv class, Chief. You're not ever supposed to say no. Now we have to start from scratch."

"You are so weird. And I'm hungry again." She turned back to the sink and fished her plate out, then brushed by him to sit at the table. "Ugh. My coffee is cold. What a waste."

"Say no more, Chief." Matt chuckled, snatching her mug off the table and dumping the contents into the sink, then filling it with the last of the steaming hot stuff in the pot. "See how good you'd have it if you gave me a chance?"

"You are only messing with me, right?" Becky's voice sounded weary. Maybe he should give it a rest.

"What do you mean?" He flipped the machine off and turned back to find her staring at him thoughtfully.

"I seriously don't have the time or energy to figure you out, Matt." She raised her eyebrows. "Like, you are only having a good time? Trying to lighten the mood?"

"Not necessarily," he said honestly. "I'm having fun. And I do tend to use humor to make hard times more bearable. But I'm entirely serious when I say there's something here." He gestured between them. "And I don't see the point in beating around the bush. We both know life is too short for that."

"I'm not going to fall for you." She stated it so matter-of-factly, he believed her.

"Don't jump to hasty conclusions," he argued anyway. "We haven't gotten to the good part yet."

She gave a weak laugh and took the coffee he held out to her. "Honestly, it's flattering. But I didn't come here to find anything more than the guys who slipped through my grasp in Yemen. Once they're neutralized, I'll be gone again."

"Long distance doesn't scare me." He could see the determination in her eyes, but it wouldn't stop him from trying.

"I'm married to my career. Just ask Rob."

"I enjoy a challenge."

She huffed in exasperation. "You're wasting your energy."

"It's mine to waste, I suppose."

Real disappointment settled in his gut for a moment. Thankfully, he had energy to spare and optimism in droves. Maybe she truly believed there wasn't a man who could crack the hard exterior around her heart, but she'd never met Matthew Taylor before—except for the one time, but she didn't remember that.

"You know . . ." He slid back into the chair across from her. "We've also got the whole grumpy-sunshine thing going too."

"You just called yourself 'sunshine.'" She looked at him like he'd opened the yellow can of skunk coffee in her face.

"And you admitted that you're grumpy."

"Guilty." She shrugged, downing more coffee. Then said, "With good reason."

"Stupid Rob." Matt sipped on his own lukewarm brew, wishing his antics had taken the furrow from her brow for a little while longer.

She was too young and too remarkable a woman to let one bad relationship put her off of the idea of love. Rebecca Salazar needed the right guy to remind her that they weren't all the same. He nearly mentioned theirs could be a second-chance romance but thought better of it.

"Yeah." She nodded, diverting her eyes to her plate. "Stupid Rob."

A strange mix of emotions filled Becky as she followed Matt's cruiser into Rosman—semi-hating that the man felt like an ally after what transpired in the cabin. She was supposed to be fully inoculated against guys like him, having spent the entirety of her career making a sport out of knocking them off their high horses. For once, she wasn't so sure of herself.

Her treacherous inner voice took full advantage of her moment of doubt, twisting scripture to fit Matt's narrative of how things would go.

Pride goes before a fall . . . right into hillbilly arms.

If she hadn't sworn off relationships, she might actually enjoy flirting with Matt. Oh, who was she kidding? She did enjoy it, but that didn't change anything. *Chief Salazar* was too good at her job, and it was too important to let herself get distracted. She wasn't capable of having a family *and* her career. She owed it to her country to stay on track and fulfill her oath to the best of her ability.

"All enemies, foreign and domestic. That's why I'm here, and that's why I'll move on to the next place."

It wasn't that Rob scared her away from attempting another relationship as much as that he had reminded her of the purpose God had placed on her life. God wouldn't have given her the abilities she possessed only for her to walk away from the responsibility of deploying them.

Becky shook the what-ifs from her mind, refocusing on her surroundings. Rosman was breathtakingly beautiful in the daytime and busier. Christmas decorations and festively-dressed pedestrians littered the small town. Worry for the smiling faces she saw along the drive made her pulse tick up. She'd lost focus this morning, letting both the banter with Matt and the ugly aside with Rob upend her equilibrium. With a deep, purposeful breath, Becky recentered herself and prepared for the task at hand.

"God, don't let these people be in danger. Let me be wrong about everything."

In her gut, she knew it wasn't that easy.

"Guide us to the answers, Lord. Show us how to stop what's coming."

She parked beside Matt in front of Rosman Town Hall—which looked way too small for the forty-eight-person task force. The fire marshal might very well shut them down. She ignored the suits standing outside the building. One of them had to be Rob, and she simply refused to look at the philanderer directly. Matt lingered at the hood of his cruiser, clearly waiting for her. Why must that put butterflies into her stomach? And furthermore, why did she enjoy their incessant fluttering?

Stop it, stop it, STOP IT!

Sliding out of her truck, she straightened her jacket and zipped it, then made her way around the truck bed. Her eyes caught on the taillight and more fluttering rippled through her torso.

By the time she reached the passenger door, Matt was already waiting by it. She diverted her eyes before they locked on his, instead opening the door to retrieve her file box.

"Let me." His hand jutted around her, grasping the box. She nearly snapped at him that she could handle it, but what was the point? He wasn't going to stop being all sweet and heroic. It was etched into his very DNA.

"Thanks." She stepped back, allowing him easier access to the box.

"Well, well, well . . ." A familiar voice rang through the air. "If it isn't the best and brightest spyglass the Navy has to offer. Somebody get the chief a bottle of water—she looks parched this far from the ocean."

Becky spun around, beaming. "Conor Flynn."

"At your service." Conor opened his arms wide.

Becky didn't hesitate to embrace her old friend. The man who towered over her and gave the best hugs seemed outside of time, not having aged a day since she met him over five years ago.

"I heard you might be hanging it up, Special Agent in Charge." Becky leaned back, only then realizing Conor didn't wear a suit. "And you're not on my contact list for this op. What are you doing here?"

Conor's brow furrowed as he released her. "Coincidence, actually. I have family in the area that I'm visiting for the holidays. A birdie told me that I should be at Town Hall this morning—in a consulting sort of capacity."

"A birdie?" Becky suppressed a sigh.

"One who happens to be flying this direction with all of his expertise in explosive ordnance disposal . . ."

Becky stood a bit straighter. "You know Sanchez?"

"We worked together once." The corners of Conor's lips pulled in slightly, not quite forming a grimace but close enough that she got the hint.

"You've seen him in action."

Conor nodded. "And he makes it a point to check in from time to time."

"That's . . . fortuitous." Becky fought the urge to warn Conor to pack his family up and get the heck out of Dodge. He had to already know what both her presence and one of the top EOD Marines would mean. But Conor had never been one to run away from danger.

Conor grunted. "Providential may be more like it."

"Yeah. Your knowledge and experience could be invaluable here." Becky jumped when someone brushed her elbow. "Oh, Special Agent Conor Flynn, this is Deputy Taylor."

"I know Matt." Conor slapped him on the arm.

"Of course you do," Becky said under her breath.

Conor grinned as he went on. "They've really assembled the A-Team, haven't they?"

"If you say so." Becky grimaced. "You haven't seen the whole crowd yet."

"Yeah, I saw enough of it. If Simms bothers you, let me know." Conor met her eyes with a pointed look. "I'm itching to knock him down a few pegs. Again."

"His very existence bothers me, Conor."

"Me too," Matt piped in. "Stupid Rob."

Conor laughed at that. "He has that effect on people."

"Shall we?" Becky gestured for Matt to lead the way and took Conor's arm when he offered it.

Conor's mere presence would irk Rob to no end. He might never admit it, but she knew it had cut Rob deeply when he lost Conor's respect. The older FBI agent was a legend and Rob's mentor for years. A better man would have tried to mend fences and pay penance for his mistakes, but not Robert Simms. Instead he had doubled down and rubbed elbows with less savory and more powerful people until he attained success through other means. The whole thing was a shining example of all that was wrong with the system and all that needed to be rectified, but that was someone else's war to wage.

Chapter 4

10:45 A.M. - ROSMAN TOWN HALL

AN OMINOUS FEELING CLUNG to the air inside Rosman Town Hall. Visually, the building was an explosion of cheer, with multiple Christmas trees and all manner of decorations strewn around the hole-in-the-wall meeting place. The room erupted with murmurs when Becky seemed to have concluded her brief. As Matt had anticipated after the spoilers Becky gave him this morning, her intel was solid, alarmingly grave, and just short of actionable. All of the human intelligence collected on the ground confirmed that *al-Qaeda* was confident in a civilian casualty count that would number in the millions. The finer details, however, seemed to be out of reach. The men in power must be keeping the full picture in a very small and impenetrable circle.

There were plans for building bombs and taking out communications, but none of it warranted the projected body count. Not in a place as remote as Rosman and the surrounding communities. Not even if they hit the entire county with a string of bombs and electromagnetic pulses. An attack like that would need to be in a densely populated area in order to achieve the projected goal. It would make more sense if they were trafficking something, like the drugs and weapons operation in Silver Ridge years ago—but an attack?

Knocking the power out would definitely make people uncomfortable, but it wouldn't kill many. Most folks had generators or fireplaces. Emergency protocols would be activated to ensure the more vulnerable of the population were brought to a central location for warmth and sustenance. Power outages were nothing they hadn't dealt with every winter since the invention of electricity. What weren't they seeing?

Something pricked at the back of Matt's mind, but he couldn't focus well enough to pinpoint what was bothering him specifically. There were too many variables missing and too little time to figure them out. If they were going to get to the heart of it, they needed to find who *al-Qaeda* had sent to their sleepy town. That should be easy enough. Like Becky, tourists, transplants, and insurgents were easy to spot. No doubt someone had already noticed strangers in the area.

"There's something else." Becky spoke above the growing tension, making an uncomfortable silence fall on the room once more. "Several Yemeni and Saudi assets seemed surprised by the target area but couldn't give actionable intel to point us in another direction. One highly trusted informant in particular was adamant that the attack was too early and too small. He said all the buzz in his sphere of influence was focused on January and the entire country. Many are calling it 'The New Year of Reckoning' . . . for infidels."

Becky gulped and studied her hands for a beat. "There's ample reason to suspect that this attack is a test run for something large-scale. Unfortunately, it's all we have to go on at the moment, and if we can't figure it out before Christmas Day, it will likely be too late to stop the larger plan from coming to fruition."

Matt clenched his fist. This felt like facing the insurgency in Niger all over again, small attacks for a much larger end game. Only Rosman didn't have preexisting instability or a power vacuum to be filled in the wake of the attack.

As with any situation involving too much brass and not enough muddy boots, the back and forth between agency heads was going nowhere fast. How was it that upward of forty people from seventeen different intelligence agencies seemed completely inept? Half of the room began fighting Becky on the way she'd divided up responsibilities, and the other half of them looked like deer in headlights. Matt waited for her to look his way and assign him a task, but she didn't. When the infighting turned to talks of restructuring the hierarchy and who should really be in charge, Matt stood up with a grunt, stomping toward the door. He needed a quiet moment to catch the breath that was being choked out of him. He hadn't made it three feet out of the building before a hand grasped his elbow.

"Matt, wait." Becky had slipped out behind him. "Where are you going?"

"Sorry, I—" He licked his lips, trying to remember why he'd abandoned his post. Oh yeah, he couldn't breathe. "I thought you didn't have a use for me yet. My skills come later, right?"

"Are you kidding?" She blinked up at him, stepping further away from the door. "You're the only one who has any real, practical experience that will come in handy here. John is right about you."

"Thanks?" Her words weren't the least bit reassuring. "That seems like an oversight."

She squeezed her eyes shut. "There's only so much I can do. I've got a six-man team arriving later today, tomorrow morning at the latest. There may be a delay."

"Another delay?"

"I'll get it sorted." Her fiery brown eyes flashed at him. "I'm getting nowhere fast in there. I handed HQ over to Homeland—mostly to tick off the FBI, but none of it matters. Conor gave me the nod."

"The nod?"

"We're going to get this done the old-fashioned way. Let those people in there believe they're running the show while the few of us that know how to take action . . . take it without asking." She glanced back at the door. "The rear admiral will have our backs. He sent me here to get the job done, knowing full well it would come to this."

"Roger." Matt scrubbed his hands over his face and took a full, deep breath. This was a plan he could live with. "What do you need from me right now?"

"Get me out of here before I throw a chair at a four-star."

He pursed his lips and nodded. Becky was funny when she wanted to be, and he didn't hate the idea of putting a few miles between them and the chaos.

"I've got your back, Chief, but what's the actual game plan?"

"We have to be back here in about two hours, preferably with some sort of progress that will prove to the rest of those yahoos how valuable we actually are in this." She huffed a breath. "Then maybe they'll shut up and listen to reason."

"Who's on your six-man team?"

"An EOD specialist—he's the real-life MacGyver of diffusing bombs, and he's a Raider like you—and several other operators I've worked with before—Rangers and a couple SEALs. They're solid, but we've got to know where to send them, and you're the key to figuring that out."

"We should have been looking for these terrorists yesterday. Last night. This morning." He said the part she left out.

"That's how it was supposed to happen." She crossed her arms. "These are the cards we've been dealt. Any ideas where to start?"

"Yeah. You know what they say about small towns." He'd smile if his anxiety wasn't spiking.

"Everybody knows everybody's business?" Becky guessed.

"And one person in particular is at the heart of it around here."

Becky didn't turn back to get her jacket from the building before she started toward his cruiser. The woman must be determined to catch pneumonia. He thought about pointing out how she couldn't take down bad guys from the hospital, but he had an extra jacket if she needed it.

"Where are you two going?" Conor Flynn emerged from Town Hall. Rob was hot on his heels, scowling at Matt.

"We're headed out to run down a lead," Becky answered, pausing in the parking lot.

"We'll come along," Rob spoke up.

"You're not invited," Becky snapped. "Conor is welcome, of course."

"Rebecca, don't be difficult." Rob narrowed his eyes. "We have to work together on this."

"Great. So get to work. I gave you an objective all your own, unless you weaseled your way out of it in there," Becky retorted. "You are NOT getting into the same vehicle as me. Besides, I know how you hate to get your shoes dirty. No telling where we'll end up today."

"You're wearing heels." Rob crossed his arms, but Becky ignored him entirely.

"You two go ahead." Conor spoke before Rob could say anything more. "Simms and I will check out another lead."

"Godspeed." Becky gave an unconvincing smile.

"Daylight's wasting, Simms." Conor winked at Becky and started walking toward Rob's SUV. "Let's see if you've forgotten everything I taught you."

Rob mumbled something as he strode past Becky. The wounded expression that flashed across her face as she turned away made Matt's stomach sour. Then she swiped a tear from her cheek right before she climbed into the cruiser. Anger coursed through him.

"What did he say to you?" Matt asked when he shut the driver's side door.

"Rob, like you, is convinced that you're my lover. It's just not so adorable when he says it."

"You think I'm adorable?" Matt grinned, ignoring the urge to follow the FBI vehicle leaving in the opposite direction.

She cleared her throat and looked out the front windshield. "Where are we headed?"

"To get some lunch." He cranked the cruiser and aimed it toward the mouth of the French Broad River. "As your lover, is it my responsibility to wipe the floor with Rob's smug face? Please say yes."

"Save that angst for the terrorists. Rob's not worth the trouble." She glanced over at Matt. "Why are we getting lunch?"

"We gotta eat, Chief." He slowed to let a cat cross the street safely. "It can be our first official date. Last night and this morning didn't count. Now that you know my intentions . . ."

"Good grief, you're like the Energizer Bunny of failed attempts."

"I prefer 'master of taking the impossible shots,' if you don't mind." He leaned toward her, smiling and resting his elbow on the center console. "It's brave, courageous . . . and endearing."

"Wow." Becky gaped at him, eyes going wide before she cleared her throat. "I'll eat because I'm hungry, but it most certainly is not a date."

"Fair enough."

"And after we eat?" She waved her hand for him to elaborate on the plans that didn't revolve around wearing her down.

"Sit back and trust me, woman."

"You are such a Neanderthal," Becky grumbled.

"I think you love it," Matt accused. "You built your career by bossing Neanderthals around."

"What's that supposed to mean?" She turned in the passenger seat, glaring at him.

"Come on, admit it. Nothing brings you more joy than pointing operators toward a threat and watching them wipe it out." He looked both ways before turning left onto the Rosman Highway. "I've seen it in your eyes."

"Oh, really? You deduced that from a single brief. That makes loads of sense."

"I didn't say I saw it today, *Stunner*." Was he really going to admit to remembering her when she clearly hadn't thought twice about him? Yes. Yes, he was. "We met once before."

"Yeah, I got the feeling . . . just can't put my finger on it." She studied the side of his face with an intensity that made his palms sweaty. His memories of that day swirled around in his mind. The same intensity on her face, the way she commanded a room full of downright lethal men—as if they were all lumps of putty in her hands—and a cute ponytail bouncing behind her head. The more functional dress of special operations, lacking enforcement of military standards, had left him no clues at all to her branch of service or rank back then.

"Where was it?" She nudged his elbow.

He cleared his throat, slowing down to turn into the parking lot of The Outfitters, where the two main highways intersected.

"Hope you like barbeque."

"Are you seriously going to ignore my question?" She crossed her arms, frowning like a toddler. "I'm not gonna budge until you answer me."

"Somalia." Heat crept up his neck after saying the single word.

"I haven't been there in . . ."

"Six years?" He glanced over, surprised to see her eyes shining with delight.

"You remember me from a single day six *years* ago?"

"You're unforgettable, babe." He winked.

"Ew. Don't call me babe."

"Noted, baby . . . beautiful . . . boss?"

"Ah!" A look of recognition spread across her face as she ignored the string of pet names. "You totally flirted with me then too. And . . . the coffee." She tossed her head back with a laugh. "You made the same quip about an M4 carbine. Oh, you really are funny."

"Yeah, I left quite an impression." He rolled his eyes. "Didn't take you long at all."

"Give me a break." Her warm smile gave him the sense he'd accomplished something by reminding her of their past connection. "Do you know how many ops I've run since then? How many cups of coffee I've been handed by hot guys?"

"You think I'm hot?"

"I think *you* think you're hot." Her cheeks flushed, prompting him to let that one slide for now.

"You're telling me I didn't stand out *at all*."

"You did, actually." She leaned against the door, still smiling. "But not because of the flirting or any of . . . this." She gestured at his whole person.

"No? Then I'm dying to know what you're smiling about."

"You guys took down the most prominent cell in the region on that op." Her smile faded slightly and she glanced at her hands folded in her lap. "They were . . . the worst kind of monsters."

The terrorist cell they'd gone up against didn't even stick out in his memory. Aside from meeting Becky, the mission wasn't much different than any other. Point, shoot, move on to the next. When he looked at her again, Becky's face had drawn into a grimace, as if she were in physical pain from whatever she was thinking about.

"We only took them out because you told us which door to kick in." He tried to draw her back into the present. After a moment, she half-smiled and nodded.

"Team effort." She bit her lip, studying his face again. "Taylor. You took out a sniper on the roof."

"I—yeah, I think I did." His own cheeks warmed under her gaze.

"And three guys along the perimeter," she added.

"That's right. How do you remember that but didn't recognize me until I spelled it out for you?"

"I associate names with stats." She covered her mouth as she snickered. "It's how my mind works. Sorry."

"It's like a flamethrower to the ego."

"I actually did recognize the scar on your cheek, but didn't really think much of it."

"Wow. The hits keep coming." He gripped his chest.

"How'd you get the scar?" She leaned forward slightly.

"Wouldn't you like to know?"

"I really would, actually." She reached up and shoved his shoulder.

"My mom . . ." He started to tell her, then thought better of it. "We had an unfortunate accident with some broken glass. It's nothing exciting like the scar on my hip."

"I'm not gonna ask to see your hip, if that's what you're smirking about." She mimicked what he assumed was her version of the look on his face. "But where'd you earn that one?"

"Kandahar."

She sighed, nodding. "Ah, the good old days. Back when it was someone else's backyard."

"Speaking of which, we'd better get to it." He paused with one foot out the door, then reached into the backseat and grabbed his extra jacket. "Here, put this on."

"You're the best boyfriend ever. Not that the bar is set high, mind you." She took the jacket, snorting when his mouth fell open. She reached a hand to his chin and pushed his mouth shut, repeating his words from breakfast. "I'm joking, Matt. Clearly."

"Too bad." He recovered from his shock.

"Thanks for the jacket. I was so keen to get away from the HQ drama, I totally left—" Her eyes went wide. "I don't have my phone." She gasped. "I don't have my wallet either."

"Oh, no!" Matt gripped her forearm. "What will you do?"

"Not eat?" She gave him a sheepish smile.

"Not an option." He shook his head. "Looks like we really are on a date, and lucky for you, I'm the best boyfriend ever."

"I'll pay you back." She didn't throw any snark his way. She must be hungry enough to ignore his antics.

"You do like barbeque, right?"

"What kind of question is that?" She hopped out of the cruiser, sliding the jacket on. His stomach took a little leap, seeing her swallowed up by a piece of his clothing.

After they'd ordered their food and found a spot to sit close to the river, Becky leveled a more serious look at him. The pleasant jaunt down lover's lane was clearly over.

"Why are we here, Matt? What is this place?"

"A hub of sorts. A lot of people pass through here, locals and tourists alike. The Outfitters carries all the necessities for . . . roughing it."

"I see." She nodded, glancing over his shoulders at something that caught her eye.

Matt turned in time to see the proprietor of the establishment walking toward them and her ugly mutt limping a few feet ahead of her.

"Bocephus!" Matt scratched the dog's salt-and-pepper neck and offered him a bite of brisket. After slightly choking on the meat, Bocephus plopped down beside the wooden picnic table with a phlegmy cough. The creature had to be nearing death. Patches of hair had fallen out in various places and didn't show signs of growing back. The poor thing ought to be put out of his misery.

"To what do I owe the pleasure of your visit, deputies?" Whit Barton kicked Matt's leg and settled on the bench next to him. The mess of blonde hair on top of her head was the same shade as his, but the family resemblance stopped there. "I've told you before, Taylor, I'm no narq. You ain't gettin' nothin' outta me."

"You just assaulted an officer of the law, dingus. You'll talk or I'll haul you in kicking and screaming." He tilted his head, leveling his most threatening stare. "And it'll be my genuine pleasure to put you where you belong."

"Matt," Becky gasped from across the table. "Take it down a notch, will you?"

"Hey, I'm just glad he's stringing sentences together now. We worried for the first couple of decades." Whit looked back at Matt. "Who's the new partner?"

"Becky, this gem of a woman is my older cousin, Whit."

"Three months, Matthew. That hardly makes me 'older.' We graduated together, for crying out loud." She scowled. "You're so full of—"

"Whit owns the place." He cut her off, then answered her question. "Becky is only borrowing my jacket because she's got a thing for me. She's not law enforcement material."

"Whit is right. You are full of it." Becky glared at him, quick to turn coats against him. "And what do you mean, I'm not law enforcement material? You're not earning any brownie points with that."

He put his hand up to hide his mouth from Whit. "She doesn't like cops. Play it cool."

"How many cousins do you have, anyway?" Becky seemed genuinely curious. "And do they own the whole town?"

"Ha!" Whit smacked Matt's arm. "Darn near half of it. What the Millers don't own anyway. Becky, you're not from around here, are ya?"

"That's the same thing Matt said yesterday." Becky looked amused. "Is it that obvious I'm an outsider?"

"Well now, let's see." Whit leaned forward, hazel eyes assessing Becky. "You look like a fed. You talk like a Yankee . . . sorta. And you're eating with Matthew Taylor. That's all pretty indicative that you don't work or live here, and you should probably disinfect yourself after wearing that jacket. Don't want to catch his particular strain of stupid—highly lethal."

"Hey, now." Matt backhanded Whit's arm, feigning hurt feelings. "No need to get quite so ugly. I'll call Granny."

"You should." Whit hit him back. "You've missed three family dinners. She's startin' ta think you don't love her anymore. We've got the Christmas potluck tomorrow. Right after church. If you miss that, I'm not sneakin' you any fruitcake. Plus, you might be uninherited . . . or is it disinherited?"

"From what?" Matt scoffed. "Granny's ceramic cat collection?"

"Hey, they could be worth somethin'." Whit shrugged. "Never know."

"I have to work tomorrow." Matt glanced up at Becky, who was silently observing the exchange. "Becky is itching to see me in action—again."

"She trying to recruit you or somethin'?" Whit looked between them. "You don't want him in the FBI, honey. He looks awful in a suit."

"Do I honestly give off FBI vibes?" Becky grimaced, glancing down at her slacks and the button-up she wore under Matt's bulky jacket. "I've got to buy new clothes."

"It's not the clothes. You dress like our Aunt Sheila, which is fine—for a bank teller." Whit lowered her voice to a whisper. "It's the hair."

Becky's hand flew to the low bun as she blinked at Whit. Was she really taking his cousin's words to heart? The woman had on fly-fishing overalls, for crying out loud. Though Matt wouldn't complain if Becky's ponytail made a comeback.

"You'uns have to be here for a reason." Whit furrowed her brow. "And don't tell me it's the food. You always take it to go and never stop in to say hey. Shameful, really, treatin' your family so poorly."

"You're hardly one to talk, Whit." He shoved her sideways. "You send me a one-finger salute every chance you get."

"I don't like your vehicle, is all." Whit shrugged. "That's on you."

"Matt." Becky raised her eyebrows. "Was there something you wanted to ask Whit?"

"Right. Have you seen anything out of the ordinary lately?" He jumped right into it. "Strangers that seemed . . . off? Anything."

"Actually, yeah." Whit leaned back like he'd slapped her. "Four sketchy looking guys came through a couple days ago. Loaded up on supplies like they were vacationing for a week or two. Didn't buy any bait. No fishing or hunting gear at all. Could be they're avid hikers. They did take a few maps . . . but they didn't have the right shoes on. I dunno, something about 'em." She shook her head. "I didn't like the look of 'em."

"What did they look like?" Becky prodded.

Whit bit down on the corner of her lip before answering. "Listen, I'm not one to discriminate. I didn't phrase that right. It's not how they *looked* or sounded, just that they were acting shifty. Glancin' over their shoulders, eyeing everybody who walked in. They seemed real nervous. Stuff like that."

"Whit, a description would be nice." Matt leaned in her direction, widening his eyes in anticipation.

"Middle Eastern?" She said it like a question, clearly worried about how she'd come across. "Honestly, I think only one of them spoke English. At least he's the only one who spoke to me and only asked where the coffee filters and phone chargers were."

"Coffee filters and phone chargers." Becky put her fork down. "That means they've got access to electricity . . . a cabin or house."

"Or a camper," Matt added.

"They'd probably trip the power in a camper. They bought every phone charger I had. Different types. Eight in all." Whit shook her head. "Isn't that nutso?"

"Yeah." Matt balled his hands into fists, trying not to react. It wasn't nutso at all, considering the men might be using phones to detonate bombs. That many chargers meant they probably had several times as many phones and bombs to go with them.

Becky had to be thinking the same thing. Her brown eyes darkened when she looked at Matt with a grim expression.

The next second, she turned to Whit, asking, "Do you happen to have cameras in the store?"

"Nope." Whit shook her head.

"Did you notice what they were driving and which way they headed?" Matt questioned.

Whit pursed her lips, pausing before she asked, "What's all of this about, Matthew?"

"You don't wanna know, Cuz. Did you see or not?"

"Yeah." She closed her eyes as if remembering. "Beat-up dark blue SUV. A Tahoe, I'm sure of it, because it reminded me of the one Joey wrecked in high school."

"So an older model?" Matt interrupted.

"Right. And they headed up toward Balsam Grove."

"That's a start." Matt sighed. "But honestly, they could have hit the Blue Ridge Parkway and be anywhere by now."

"No. If these are our guys, they're close." Becky stared at her half-eaten plate of brisket. "We've got to find that Tahoe. Can you put out an APB or whatever?"

"It's like one second she is a cop . . . and the next she isn't." Whit eyed Becky suspiciously. "Who are you exactly?"

Becky swallowed hard. "Not the person you wanna see in your hometown. Think of me as a stalker . . . of creeps."

"That's not at all cryptic." Whit raised an eyebrow, turning to Matt. "Do I need to get Granny out of town for a while or what?"

"I'll . . . let you know." Matt diverted his gaze.

Becky cleared her throat and widened her eyes. Matt shrugged, shooting her a "come on, it's my family" look. She shook her head and sighed.

Whit stood and took a step back toward her store. "See you tomorrow? Even if it's just to grab a to-go plate. You gotta eat." Bocephus grunted as he moved to follow Whit. "We . . . we asked Penny to come."

Matt hesitated, unable to form his response.

"He'll be there," Becky answered for him.

Whit chuckled, tucking a strand of loose blonde hair behind her ear. "I like you, Becky. Why don't you come along too? Granny will be tickled pink to meet Matt's new lady friend."

Whit scurried off before Becky could respond.

"You brought that on yourself," he taunted. "And you have to go."

"Do not." Becky picked up her plate and took a bite of brisket.

"Do too. You don't turn down an invitation in these parts if you want to stay in the good graces of the locals, aka your informants. Besides, Granny lives in Balsam Grove. We can go early and search for that Tahoe. I know which houses sit empty—there's only a handful—so it's actually perfect."

"Riddle me this: how is it that I can't turn down an invitation to lunch"—Becky jabbed her forkful of brisket at him, leaning forward—"when you've missed the last three dinners?"

"I'm family. The black sheep of it, at that." He sat up straight, grinning ear to ear. "It's what's expected of me."

"Oh, please."

"What's expected of *you* is to show up on my arm and be sweet to my granny." He pursed his lips. "Now that I say that out loud, maybe I should make your apologies instead."

"You don't think I'm capable of being nice to your granny?" She threw a pickle slice at his face, shocking him when it ricocheted off his cheek and fell to the ground.

"I don't think 'nice' is in your wheelhouse, Chief." He threw an onion slice from his own untouched plate, missing on purpose. "You're a self-proclaimed grump, after all."

Becky poked another piece of brisket with her fork, dipped it in sauce, and held it up with a threatening look in her eyes.

"You wouldn't." He prepared to leap from the bench if she made like she would.

Shoving the bite in her mouth, she spoke around the food. "No, I wouldn't waste good brisket on the likes of you."

"You're so ungrateful. I'm the best boyfriend ever, I bought you that brisket out of the goodness of my heart, and this is how you treat me?"

"Aren't you going to eat yours?"

He took a bite to appease her, only then realizing how hungry he was.

After he'd taken a couple more bites, Becky cleared her throat and asked, "Who's Penny?"

Matt kept chewing, buying himself a few seconds and wishing she hadn't picked up on that bit of information.

"My mother," he finally answered.

"Oh." Her face brightened with what might actually be mischief. "I didn't realize you'd be introducing me to your mom so soon."

Her smile faded when he took another bite instead of responding.

He swallowed and cleared his throat, determined to maneuver into a new subject. "Who did you think Whit was talking about?"

"I was worried about one of your exes meandering in and thickening the plot." She rolled her eyes dramatically. "Wasn't that obvious?"

"I can't tell if you're joking or not," he admitted, hoping she'd give him a clue.

She only shrugged, enjoyment lighting her eyes.

"I don't really have any exes, just so you know."

"I'm not buying it." Becky shook her head. "You're too big a flirt to make a claim like that."

"I only flirt with truly stunning women," he said honestly. "Those are few and far between."

"How few?" She narrowed her eyes.

"I've searched the globe and only ever found one." He shoved his last bite into his mouth and grinned in satisfaction.

"Oh, you are good," she whispered.

"So, tomorrow?" He held his breath.

"I'd have gone simply to watch Whit take more jabs at you, but the thought of meeting Granny and seeing her ceramic cat collection too?" She let out a low whistle. "That's too good a chance to pass up."

"You're only going to hunt for creeps. I see right through you."

"Maybe." The glint in her eyes made him think he might be a little bit wrong. "You'd better pick me up by daybreak . . . if we don't locate the Tahoe today. There's no way I'm sitting on that information until morning."

"Man, I am good at my job," Matt pointed out. "You're going to give me all the credit, right?"

"Of course not—this was all me."

"How do you figure? One five-minute conversation with the first informant on *my* list, and I got better intel than you could have hoped for."

"It was my idea." She squared her shoulders. "I know how to best deploy my assets."

She must've realized her mistake a moment later. She instantly cut him off before he could say a single word about her assets.

"Don't do it." She shook her head. "It's the lowest of low-hanging fruit. I don't want to lose that much respect for you."

"Tell me I'm the best, Chief. Just a little bit of praise, and I'll forget all about your as—"

"Great work, Taylor." She spoke over him. "You're the most valuable member of the team."

"Why, thank you, Chief." He placed his hand over his heart. "You don't know how much it means to hear you say so."

"Don't look so satisfied with yourself, *Sergeant* Taylor." Becky folded her empty plate in half and stood up.

"I picked up staff sergeant before I got out, actually."

"Aha!" She tossed the plate into a trashcan behind him. "Told you I'd figure it out. And I totally outrank you."

Matt chuckled in spite of himself. He'd walked right into her trap.

Chapter 5

12:15 P.M. - ROSMAN TOWN HALL

WHEN BECKY CLIMBED OUT of Matt's cruiser, leaving the deputy to finish reporting the blue Tahoe, Conor immediately stepped away from a group of agents he'd been talking to outside of HQ, making a beeline for her.

"Where have you two been?" The worry etched on his face sent a shooting pain into her stomach. "I texted you twenty minutes ago."

"I haven't seen the text." Becky could kick herself for leaving her phone and couldn't bring herself to admit to the misstep.

"Yeah, service is spotty in these parts." Conor shrugged.

She wasn't about to outright lie to the man, so she said, "We found a solid lead. Matt is putting out an APB on a suspicious vehicle now."

"We got something too." Conor jerked his head toward the group gathered by the door. "Let's see if our two puzzle pieces add up to disaster."

Becky waved for Matt to meet them inside, turning toward Town Hall. She ignored the sour look on Rob's face until he blocked the doorway.

"Move." She looked him dead in the eye.

"We need to clear the air." He didn't budge.

A warm hand landed on the small of her back.

"Is there a problem, Bobby?" Matt's voice reverberated through her when he spoke.

"It's Special Agent Simms, crayon eater." Rob's face reddened.

Matt obviously held in a laugh before saying, "My apologies, *Special* Agent Simms. I'll ask again, is there a problem?"

"Yeah. I'm trying to have a private conversation with—"

The door opened, hitting Rob on the arm and making him jump out of the way.

"No time for chitchat." Becky took her opportunity and bolted around the exiting Sheriff Woodhouse into the cover of Town Hall. Matt could handle Rob, she had no doubt.

"Everybody quiet down. We really don't have time to waste," Conor was saying when she stepped into the area they'd turned into the task force headquarters, grabbing her phone and sighing in relief.

She'd only missed Conor's text and one from the rear admiral reassuring her he'd handle any backlash from whatever action she took on the ground.

Conor continued, "I've got new information, and so does Chief Salazar. Chief?"

He gestured for Becky to speak first, taking a seat on the front row as she moved to the head of the room. Matt slipped inside ahead of Rob, who was shooting daggers at the back of his head.

Yeesh.

"A local business owner sold camping supplies to four men believed to be Middle Eastern. They left her location in a beat-up older model Tahoe, dark blue. They drove in the direction of Balsam Grove, which is about ten miles northwest of our current location, on Parkway Road or Highway 215." Becky gestured to Matt. "Deputy Taylor has alerted local and state law enforcement to be on the lookout for the vehicle, with instructions to observe and report but not to engage the men. We need to know where they're working from and try to find whatever additional intel we can."

Becky took a deep breath before concluding, "We do believe them to be inside a structure with electricity due to the purchase of coffee filters and *eight* phone chargers, which is further confirmation that they're building improvised explosive devices—a lot of them. That's what I have at this time. I'll turn it over to Special Agent Flynn."

Conor stood and patted her on the shoulder as she moved to take the seat he'd vacated.

"Unfortunately, that information fits all too well with my own. Four men buying concentrated ammonium nitrate fertilizer. So far, we've confirmed the same description—always two to four men, described as being Middle Eastern—purchasing whatever each feed and supply store had on hand at the time. Small amounts that so far add up to just under one hundred bags. That's at least four thousand pounds."

Gasps sounded around the room.

"It seems they've bought up everything they could find in the tri-county area. We can expect that they're building several smaller explosives, like the previous intel suggests, but we have to also be prepared for the possibility of one MacDaddy of a blast." Conor sat on the edge of the table in the front of the room. "Any which way you shake it, it's exactly what we feared. Three of the store owners we spoke with have cameras that should show footage of the men. We hope to have identities and aliases by the end of the day."

"What are we waiting for?" someone called from the back. "Let's hit the pavement."

Becky stood up and lifted her hands in front of her. "I agree we need to move on the intel and locate the terrorists posthaste. However, the last thing we want is to have these guys scatter like cockroaches. So far, we know the timeline. We have a general location. We know we're dealing with some sort of deployment of IEDs." Becky glanced at Matt. "What we need now is someone who knows the area and exactly how to blend in. We'll have a team of operators here by tomorrow. In the meantime, I'm putting Deputy Taylor—that is, Marine Special Operations Staff Sergeant Taylor—at the tip of the spear."

Voices started to rise from all around the room, bringing her authority and judgment into question once again, but Becky spoke over them.

"Taylor was born and raised right here. He faced this sort of enemy on countless ops throughout his career as a Raider. He knows how they think, move, and fight." She raised her own eyebrows at the words she spoke next. "I can't imagine there's a single operator who is more qualified to lead this mission even when the rest of the team arrives. And if you take issue with that, tell it to Rear Admiral Polken of the United States Navy."

No one argued then, which was probably due more to the admiral's reputation than anything she'd said about Matt. The Marine-turned-deputy made his way to stand beside her then. He didn't appear to be thrilled with his sudden promotion, but the firm set of his jaw told her he'd get the job done.

"Anyone who has applicable combat experience, meet me at the back of the room." He started to walk away, then paused. "That is, anyone who's actually disarmed an ordnance, cleared a compound, or been in a firefight during the global war on terror."

A few of the men grimaced and sat back down. Conor followed Matt toward the back, which was interesting. If he had war stories, he'd never shared them with her—though he had served in the Air Force before joining the FBI. Becky watched as three other men and two females made their way toward Matt.

Rob's throat clearing beside her made Becky's stomach twist into knots.

"What?" She ground the word out, thankful no one was looking their way.

"You loved that, didn't you?" Rob crossed his arms, standing shoulder to shoulder with her. "Putting the spotlight on your boyfriend right in front of me. Handing a grunt the lead on this."

"You have some serious nerve, Robert." She shook her head. "Believe it or not, this threat has nothing to do with you. It wasn't concocted just for you to get whatever you came here for. Your lack of professionalism will get people killed if you're not careful."

"My lack of professionalism? That's rich." He turned toward her. "Or do I need to remind you about this morning?"

"What about this morning?"

"He was in your cabin, Becks. He made you breakfast." Rob actually looked hurt when she turned to glare at him. "Was he in your bed before that? What's the trick exactly? Combat boots?"

Becky's hand landed hard on Rob's cheek before she could process what a colossal misstep it was. She blinked against the burn at the back of her eyes. The slap had echoed so loudly, it drew the attention of every person in the room. To their credit, no one said a word, but the move would cost her more of their trust. Why did she continue to let Rob get under her skin after all this time?

"He fixed a blown taillight on my truck." She fought to keep her voice quiet enough that no one else could hear. "All he got in return was a cup of coffee and an entertaining story about *you*."

Rob stared at her, unflinching as his cheek reddened with her handprint. "You expect me to believe he's nothing more than your errand boy? I see the way he looks at you."

"The fact of the matter is that you invented every one of the lies you have ever believed about me. I'm as pure as the driven snow when it comes to what you're insinuating, and I thank God every day that I didn't give you what you never valued in the first place."

She refused to be the one to walk away, and after five eternal seconds, Rob backed up and turned toward the exit.

Becky swallowed the emotions that had risen to her throat, turning her back on the faces in the room. Humiliation washed over her. She had to get a grip on the situations that kept distracting from the mission. Not only Rob, but Matt too. Neither of the men were focusing like they should. She'd never forgive herself if a single person died because of her.

The woodsy scent she'd already committed to memory after riding in Matt's cruiser and wearing his jacket for half an hour wafted over her shoulder. He cleared his throat behind her and barely touched her arm before she turned and purposefully moved away from his hand.

"What's your plan?" She glanced several feet behind him instead of meeting his eyes. Conor was studying her intently, but everyone else in the room seemed to have moved on from the drama.

"These people say they have experience, so why is it they can't even grasp a simple strategy, Becky? I don't trust any of them with more than observation, assuming we can locate the targets." Matt squared his shoulders. "I'd be better off going after these guys alone than trusting the available backup."

"No." She shook her head. "That's not an option. You at least have to take me with you. I can blend in."

"And if we have to engage the targets for some reason? Are you ready to be in a firefight in those heels?"

"You know I have other shoes." She set her jaw. "It won't come to that. Real backup will be here by morning."

"So you say."

"What's that supposed to mean?" She'd slap him as hard as she'd slapped Rob. "What if they don't—"

"They. Will. Be. Here," she hissed through gritted teeth.

"And what if I don't want to work with them? Maybe they're no better than the people in this room." He stepped closer, lowering his voice to a whisper. "I have to know I can trust the guys at my back, even if it's a smaller team and even if you don't like it."

"I take it back." She shook her head. "Putting you in charge was the worst idea I've had in years."

"Be serious, Salazar." The way he said her name hit like a fist to the gut.

She fumed, biting her tongue hard before asking, "What is it that you want from me, Taylor?"

His lack of confidence was shredding through her patience faster than Hillary Clinton disposed of evidence. So much for him having her back.

"I want to loop in Conor's brothers." Matt's lips set in a firm line.

"Civilians? That's your idea of a better plan?" She blinked, processing his words. She didn't know exactly what she'd expected him to say, but that wasn't it.

"Veterans, Becky. And ones that I know and trust." Matt took a deep breath. "They're the closest thing to additional boots we can get in a pinch, and they know the area just as well as I do. We need to be ready to move, with or without the guys you've got coming."

She let the request marinate in her frazzled brain, looking back at Conor to see him still studying her for what she now understood was her reaction.

"Do his brothers have more experience than the options you turned down in this room?" She didn't like the proposed idea, but she did trust Conor's judgment. This whole irritating argument could have been avoided if it had come from Conor in the first place.

"Kael served eight years in the Marine Corps, and Declan was a PJ—which you know is invaluable if, God forbid, someone gets hurt." Matt blinked in confusion. "I thought you and Conor went way back."

"We do, sort of . . . I don't remember him ever mentioning his brothers were military, let alone one being special forces." She straightened her posture. "Okay. Call them. But we aren't meeting them here. The last thing I need is for anyone in this room to catch wind of it."

Chapter 6

1:00 P.M. - THE CABIN

"It's uncanny, right?" Matt whispered, leaning close to Becky as they stared at Conor and his brothers standing under the gazebo near Becky's cabin.

Her whole demeanor had shifted after whatever transpired between her and Rob at HQ. The way Matt fumbled things right after that only added fuel to the fire. The rigid chief was back in full force. Matt got the sense all manner of pleasantries between them were over, which was probably for the best at this point. The flirting had to stop if they were both going to stay on task.

"Like clones." Becky stepped forward when the three Flynns started walking toward them.

"They're up to speed." Conor took a deep breath, hands landing on his brothers' backs with a clap.

"If you need us, we're in." Kael nodded, his expression passive. He was a Marine through and through, but Matt knew his friend didn't relish the idea of ever going back into battle. He'd put war behind him and settled into a simple, quiet life with his wife and kids.

Declan had kept at least one toe in the action since the day he'd separated from the Air Force's Special Operations Command. When he wasn't contracted on private rescue missions recovering victims of human trafficking, he led search and rescue teams across the Appalachian Mountains, fighting the elements and saving people from a different sort of peril.

"I'd like to be there, no 'ifs' about it." Declan shot a hopeful smile at Becky, then gestured over his shoulder. "I've got my gear in the truck now."

"Thanks." Becky's response came out in a sigh. "First, we need to locate the four men. Then we can talk about the best way to take them down, preferably without getting blown to smithereens in the process."

Her phone buzzed in her hand, drawing her attention away from the men.

"This might all have been for nothing." She looked back up, pocketing her phone as tension seemed to melt off of her. "All six of my guys showed up at HQ."

Declan crossed his arms with a huff.

"Conor told you both that all of this is—"

"Classified," Kael and Declan said at the same time.

"Don't worry about us running our mouths," Declan went on. "Or running for the hills. Unless the terrorists are in the hills, in which case . . ."

"We get it." Matt chuckled. "You want in on the action. And I'm not counting you out of it, no matter who is waiting at HQ."

He ignored the irritated huff that came from where Becky stood beside him. Maybe her guys were top tier, but he didn't know them, and they didn't know this area like the men standing right in front of her. This wasn't the Middle East, and there was no way Becky could deny the value the Flynn brothers would bring to the mission. She just needed time to lick the wound he'd inflicted by questioning her authority.

"If you need me," Declan confirmed. "Mind you, there's no such thing as too many medics."

"Conor?" Becky planted her hands on her hips.

"He's not going to get in the way." Conor backhanded Declan's chest. "He has a superman complex, is all."

"True." Declan shrugged and puckered his lips, taking full ownership of the accusation.

"Okay. I need to head back to HQ and then . . ." She half-turned toward Matt. "I won't be able to sit still. Is there a chance we could head up toward Balsam Grove and scope out some of those abandoned places you mentioned?"

"You're asking?" He really ought to stop popping off at the mouth. She obviously wasn't in the mood. Becky only narrowed her eyes. "That is, you read my mind, Chief."

Matt started toward his cruiser, Conor and Becky falling into step with him.

"Should I come along?" Declan called after them.

"Go home, Dec. I'll keep you posted," Conor sighed, climbing into the passenger seat when Becky silently slipped into the back. Once he shut the door, he turned toward her, saying, "Sorry about Dec. He's a bit excitable."

"It's good we have options," was all that Becky said. Her curt tone made it sound more like the entire ordeal had been a huge waste of their time.

The five minutes it took to return to HQ were filled with Conor spouting off theories that barely registered in Matt's mind. Every time he glanced at Becky in the rearview, her shoulders seemed to move closer to her ears. She started trying to exit the cruiser before he put it in park, then snarled under her breath as she seemed to remember she'd have to wait for him to open the door.

Conor walked ahead as Matt let Becky out of the cruiser. She stepped around him without a word until he grasped her wrist, asking, "You good, Chief?"

"I'm fully functional. I'll be *good* when this is over." She attempted to pull away, but he didn't release her. "We need to get inside, Taylor. The sooner we make sure everything is on track here, the sooner we can start looking in Balsam Grove. How much daylight is left, anyway?"

He let go of her then. "About four hours."

"We leave here in twenty minutes. Even if I have to hand everything over to Rob." She said his name like a curse word.

"The altercation with Rob . . . Is that what has you so upset?" Matt didn't know what to make of the emotions that paraded across her face. Anger, confusion, and maybe a flash of hurt.

"Partly." She nodded, not meeting his eyes.

"And partly me." He had to ball his hand into a fist to keep from forcing her to look at him again. He sent up a silent prayer for God to give him the right words. "I didn't mean to step on your authority. I—"

"You think I care about authority?" There was the pained look in her eyes again, only this time it didn't go away. "Matt, I'm not like the people inside that building. I don't care about anything but stopping terrorists from hurting people. But I'm not used to working with people who don't trust my judgment."

He swallowed hard. Trust was huge in her line of work. It was the difference between mission success and failure.

"I came here expecting it, sure. And I don't care if those people believe in me or my intel, so long as they don't get in my way." She hugged herself and squinted at him. "But you—"

Her words cut off like a radio losing power. Yesterday, he could have argued that he didn't know her all that well, but it wasn't that simple now. Between her reputation and his experience, there was an established level of trust that few people outside of special operations could comprehend.

"Becky, I do trust you," he said firmly.

"No." She shook her head. "Not fully, and it's okay. You weren't wrong to want Conor's brothers on board, but my guys are equally important and needed here. They aren't the enemy."

"I know." His chest tightened, knowing that the extra moisture in her brown eyes was because of him. "I'm sorry. I do trust your judgment, abilities, and experience. I shouldn't have called it into question, and I'm not questioning it now."

She nodded and turned, pausing with her hand on the door and the smallest of smiles on her lips. "I'm glad we hashed that out. I was really dreading giving you the silent treatment when we go hunting."

"Ten miles feels like thirty on these mountain roads." Becky groaned, trying to ignore the motion sickness threatening to incapacitate her. "Remind me why we had to take my truck? I think this might have been more bearable in the cruiser."

"Less conspicuous." Matt slowed down, taking yet another sharp curve.

"This thing is more red than Santa's sleigh, Taylor," she grumbled. "I wouldn't call it inconspicuous."

"You're looking a little green, Chief. Need me to pull over?"

"There's nowhere *to* pull over." She covered her mouth with her hand. "I'm fine. Stop slowing down."

"I thought sailors were immune to motion sickness."

"Maybe the ones who actually spend their days on the water are." Becky groaned again.

This feeling wasn't going to relent until she got out of the truck. Maybe she should roll the window down. The button didn't work at all when she pressed it, of course. Why hadn't she rented something shiny and brand new? Oh, right. The Asheville airport had zero rentals available at the last minute—five days before Christmas. She'd found this hunk of junk online, and the seller knocked three hundred dollars off when she told him she'd pay in cash.

The drive to Balsam Grove might actually be beautiful if it didn't make her want to lose what was left of the brisket she'd eaten several hours ago. The thought that they would be driving back down the mountain before she could collapse onto the bed in her cabin sent a throbbing sensation into her head. Her mouth began to water, and the single curve they were trapped in went on for so long, she thought the front of the truck might touch the back before they straightened out. It was the last straw.

"I'm not fine." She shook her head.

Just in the nick of time, a straightaway opened up and an extra-large gravel shoulder appeared on the right. Matt jerked the truck off the road, slamming to a halt as Becky swung the door open. The gust of cold air on her face immediately helped to tamper the nausea, but not enough to stop her from spewing the contents of her stomach into the small ditch beyond the gravel. When she was sure that she wouldn't puke again, she stumbled back and leaned on the side of the truck. Matt got out and came around to check on her. With pursed lips, he leaned one elbow on the truck bed and held a bottle of water out.

"I'm never eating barbecue again," she rasped, snatching the water from his hand.

"I definitely won't be asking for a kiss even though this is our second date," he quipped.

"Don't do that." She didn't have the energy to deal with his persistence. "You can't keep crossing that line."

"I know." He shook his head as if chiding himself internally. "I'm sorry."

Taking a big sip of water, Becky swished it around and spit it out, then took a drink that soothed her raw throat on the way down. She turned toward Matt with every intention of saying they should get back in the truck. What she saw behind him made her breath catch in her throat.

Grabbing a fistful of the flannel shirt he'd changed into, she looked him square in the eyes and said, "Act natural."

"How else would I act? Why are you—"

"I mean do not look at the Tahoe that's passing us in a couple of seconds. Not until it's in front of us."

Matt lifted his hands up to frame her face, tucking flyaway strands of hair back behind her ears. His fingertips pressed into the tense muscles at the base of her skull at the same time his thumb lightly brushed along her jaw.

"Is this natural?" he whispered, leaning close to her ear so that she had a full view of the Tahoe as it drove by.

"It's them." She narrowly avoided making eye contact with the man in the passenger seat. "It's got to be."

"Let's roll." Matt released her once the Tahoe was past them, but he didn't move more than one step away. He glanced down at her hand, still with a death grip on his shirt.

"Sorry." She ripped her hand away, jumping back like the shirt had zapped her with a jolt of electricity. "Can you tail them without tipping them off?"

Matt shot her a look of disgust, mumbling, "Can I tail them . . ."

They slammed both truck doors at the same time, Matt slinging gravel a second later.

"We should call it in." Becky's hands shook, still holding the bottle of water.

"Won't do any good in this spot." Matt's thumb tapped the steering wheel over and over. "No service. It might pick back up after a ways, but it'll be spotty."

"That's inconvenient. Hopefully they'll have the comms set up at HQ by morning," Becky grumbled, straining to see a sliver of the back of the Tahoe. "Don't lose them."

A whoosh of air came out of Matt. "You are such a control freak."

"Please don't pick a fight right now. I'm already on edge."

"No joke." He glanced over at her for a second before his eyes returned to the road ahead. "They can only go so fast on this road without wrecking, and there's nowhere to turn off this stretch. Take a breath, Chief."

She followed his advice, not feeling better until she'd digested his words. As they sat in silence, her mind flashed back to the moment she had a clear view of the Tahoe's front seat passenger. There was no question—he looked Yemeni. Actually, he looked familiar. No doubt she'd seen his face at some point. Maybe in the background of a photo or on surveillance videos the week before the Rangers moved in on the compound in Yemen. Had they missed capturing the four men by days or mere hours? They might have stopped these guys from ever getting so close to carrying out their jihad on American soil. Was it her fault? Could she have acted on intel sooner?

Becky took another deep breath, reminding herself there was still time. They had eyes on the terrorists now, and all four men would be dead or in custody by the end of tomorrow as long as they didn't lose them.

"I've got to get a bit closer." Matt interrupted her thoughts. She could see the back of the Tahoe entirely now, and Matt was slowly gaining on it.

"Don't spook them. You're getting too close."

"They're the ones slowing . . ." Matt took a deep breath, maintaining his speed. "If I slow down too much, that's equally suspicious."

"They'll see us, Matt." Becky instinctively reached for his shoulder.

"They're turning." He shrugged her hand away. "I know where they're going."

The Tahoe disappeared down an overgrown side road, and Matt flew right past it.

"You're not following them?" She strained to look back for another glimpse of the Tahoe, but it was out of sight.

"That's a dead end driveway." Matt moved his foot to the brake and stopped in the road, then backed the truck into the cover of some brush and trees. They *just* had a view of the driveway the men had gone down. "There's only two houses. One of them is sometimes used as a vacation rental—when the owner is running low on funds."

"That's good, right?" Becky studied the side of Matt's neck. He had it craned to look back the way they'd come and his carotid artery was visibly racing, splotches of red creeping up out of his collar.

"No, it's really not." His knuckles were white from gripping the steering wheel. Becky nearly yelped when his left hand suddenly hit the door and he swore under his breath, mumbling something about it being all his fault.

"Matt?"

"I'm sorry." He relaxed into the seat, scrubbing his hands over his face and into his thick hair. When he spoke again, his voice was hoarse. "I know the layout of the house. I handed my dad the nails when he built it. The owner can't possibly know who she rented it to."

"Who owns it?"

"Penny." He took a deep breath before finally looking over at Becky.

"Your mom?" she gasped.

"She lives in the other house."

"Okay." Becky's mind raced with the risks and options ahead of them. "We need to call her and get her out of there, now."

Matt was already shaking his head. "She doesn't have a phone. Regardless, she's not going anywhere."

"Why? Matt, if you tell her the dangers . . ."

He let out a bitter laugh under his breath. "Of course this is how it's going down." He met Becky's eyes. "She's nuts, Becky. Legitimately certifiable. And I'm the last person she'll listen to."

"Can you at least try?" She felt bad for the guy, but surely he wanted to get his mom to safety.

He shook his head again. "I look like my dad. She hates Dad. It's not an option, okay?"

"They're leaving the driveway. The blinker is directed this way." Becky slapped his shoulder and Matt threw the truck in reverse, pulling further off the road and jerking the wheel so they disappeared and couldn't see if or when the Tahoe passed. After several seconds, Matt inched forward, creeping toward the road. It was completely clear in both directions.

"Do you think they saw us?" Becky asked.

"Hope not."

"What's up that way?" She gestured in the direction they'd been headed before stopping.

"Balsam Grove," Matt responded flatly.

"You mean to tell me we still haven't made it there?"

That got him to almost chuckle convincingly, despite all that was going on. He pulled onto the road and drove without getting into a hurry.

"Are we trying to catch up to them?" Becky didn't know what she hoped he would say in reply.

"I . . . dunno if we should. We know where they're staying, at least." Matt pointed straight ahead. "You might have enough service to make a call in a minute."

"Matt, about Penny—"

"I'll figure it out." He cut her off. "Please . . . don't mention to anyone that she's my mom. Not unless you have to."

After driving through Balsam Grove—supposedly—and on and on for miles, Becky had lost hope that they'd spot the Tahoe again. She never could get a call out to Conor, and the text update she'd sent was still attempting to go through.

"There." Matt's voice was loud in the cab after neither of them had spoken for a full five minutes. "Why would they come here?"

Becky spotted the Tahoe on the side of the road next to a Subaru with more colorful stickers than a kindergarten classroom.

"What is this place?"

"Summey Cove Trail. They must be going to Courthouse Falls." He threw his right hand up in exasperation. "Are they seriously taking time to see the sights before they start blowing things up?"

"Maybe it's a rendezvous point . . . meeting whoever owns the other car. Or they've got something hidden up here?"

"I doubt the tree hugger who owns that Subie has any business with our guys." He pulled off the road after a short distance when the Tahoe was out of sight.

"Do you know the person who owns that car? You sound like such a jerk. Calling someone a tree hugger for driving a Subaru . . ."

"There was literally a sticker that said, 'I love hugging trees.'" Matt scowled at her. "You know, for someone whose entire job is attention to detail, you miss a lot."

Becky opened her mouth to really let him have it, then snapped it shut. He had to be going out of his mind with worry for his mom and everyone else that he loved. He'd said he trusted her. It was time to return the favor.

"You're right. They're probably not meeting the tree hugger. Let's focus on what we know." She pointed at the forest. "There are terrorists in these woods."

"This is a popular hiking destination." Matt's eyebrows knit together. "Why would they risk being seen on a busy trail?"

"Is it really busy this time of year? And this close to dusk?" Becky looked back in the direction of the trailhead. "How long is the hike?"

"Right at two miles—if they go all the way to the falls. Under an hour for an average hiker." Matt licked his lips. "There's enough daylight left. We should follow them in."

"What?" Becky's heart sped at the suggestion. "You want to risk meeting those guys on a remote trail just before dark? No way."

"There's a reason they're out here." He hesitated. "You should stay in the truck. I can probably catch up to them if I move fast, and I know how to avoid being seen. If there's any trouble here, hightail it back to HQ without me."

"No." Becky grabbed his forearm. "It's not worth the risk."

"I'll be fine." He rolled his eyes.

"I mean it's not worth tipping them off. What if they do see you and recognize you from the side of the road, or they saw the truck back there and only stopped here to see if we'd follow?" Becky shook her head. "We can't risk it. If they get skittish, there's no telling what they'll do. They could move up the attack or scatter and regroup for a later date . . ."

"Becky." His jaw was set, and she could see the resolve flashing in his eyes. "I'm going in there. I'm getting eyes on these—"

"Fine. Then so am I. It'll look more natural for a couple to be hiking together than for a random dude to be alone." She moved to get out of the truck, but Matt grabbed her shoulder. "Don't argue with me, Matt. You won't understand what they're saying even if you get close. I have to go."

"I was only going to say that nothing about your clothes will look natural on that trail."

Becky glanced down at herself. "Right. I'll change."

"You have a change of clothes in here?" Matt sat back, eyeing her doubtfully.

"Always." She stared right back. "I have a toothbrush too."

He pursed his lips, and she instinctively smacked his arms.

"And no, I'm not going to brush my teeth just so you can ask for that kiss."

"Be that way." He finally had a small smile pulling at his lips again.

Chapter 7

3:40 P.M. - PISGAH NATIONAL FOREST

STANDING AT THE BACK of Becky's truck, staring at the woods with jihadists traipsing through them, Matt sent up his tenth silent prayer since the morning brief. He needed God's guidance on so many things. Two days ago, he was content with his life. Fine with being single, resigned to his estrangement from Penny, and happy with his quiet job in his quaint little town. Rebecca Salazar was like a sandstorm, blowing into his life and obliterating his contentment.

If bachelorhood was God's plan, he'd have to accept it. But the fact that women like Becky were out there set off a desire he wasn't sure he could stamp out. Really, who did he think he was kidding? It wasn't women *like* Becky. It was her. She was one of a kind—his kind.

He couldn't shake the thought that if he'd tried harder to reconcile with Penny or get her the help she needed, she never would have been in the position to rent out her house to the most dangerous sort of characters. His muscles tensed with a wave of anger. Who was he more upset with? Himself or his enemy?

Being on the task force, tailing the terrorists, and navigating all the obstacles that loomed right in front of them should make him grateful for the changes he'd made in his life, but if he were being honest, it did the opposite. He missed the rush of barreling full speed into a firefight and going head to head with real evil. He still remembered the smell and taste of it.

Matt shook the thoughts from his head. He was confusing what he knew to be true with what the rose-hued memories were trying to make him believe. Time and distance played tricks on a man. Firefights meant watching your brothers die right beside you, sometimes for no greater purpose than to feed the military-industrial gods. Real evil existed everywhere, and it was up to good men to find it and eradicate it. Jihadists were easy to condemn, but they weren't a greater evil than the murderers, rapists, and corrupt politicians hiding in plain sight all over the world. Just last month, the sheriff's department helped root out a pedophile in the community. Wasn't that equally important? It was to the kids whose innocence wouldn't be ripped away in the future.

Maybe it was human nature to gloss over the small victories and ignore the cumulative effects that everyday actions had on one's community, country, and world. Making a difference didn't need to leave him exhausted or bleeding for it to be real. Honestly, if he'd made the difference he'd wanted to achieve when he wore a Raider patch on his arm, he wouldn't be facing the same enemy in the here and now. Furthermore, if he were still fighting on foreign soil, exactly who would be standing in the gap between his neighbors and the four guys from Yemen?

God, forgive me for questioning the path you've set for me.

Taking Becky into the woods might be his worst idea yet. He had his gun, of course, and she had hers, but no one back at HQ knew where they were. He honestly wasn't convinced he could manage staying covert on some parts of the hike—especially with her there—and she was right about the risk of tipping off the terrorists or spooking them into changing their plans. Maybe he'd been too hasty. They should pack it up and head straight back to HQ.

"Ready." Becky's statement behind his back made him nearly jump out of his tactical pants. "I did brush my teeth, but don't get any ideas about it."

"I'm starting to rethink this plan, to tell you the truth . . ."

"Don't even try it." She leveled a no-nonsense stare straight into his soul. "You were right. This is a unique opportunity, and we can't pass it up. We're going."

"You should bring your Glock," he reminded her.

"What makes you think I don't have my weapon?" She looked at him like he was the biggest idiot on the planet.

Her "change of clothes" was convincing enough. She looked like a runner aside from the Navy-issue combat boots on her feet. Those were not ideal if they were seen, but at least she wouldn't twist an ankle along the way. Wherever she'd put her Glock, it was well concealed. He was only looking for the gun in order to be thorough, of course, not to take in every inch of her in the new fabric. Her hoodie hugged her figure, which was nothing he'd complain about, but *she* might be complaining about the cold before they made it back to the truck.

She stepped around him and put some of his thoughts into words. "Stop ogling me, Taylor. I don't have a heavy jacket, and it's getting colder by the minute. Let's move fast."

"Slow is smooth, smooth is—"

"Oh no, you don't," she growled back at him. "Don't you dare appropriate a SEAL mantra, you dirty Raider."

"Roger that, Chief." He laughed, chiding himself for admiring her legs, which were way more fun to look at in the tight leggings than her dress pants. "Let's cut through the woods here to avoid being seen if someone stayed back in the Tahoe."

"Good thinking." Becky let him lead the way, following closely as he forged a shortcut to the trail.

Neither of them spoke until they finally found the worn path that led to Courthouse Falls. The air seemed weighted with the threat they both knew lay somewhere between them and the waterfall. When they'd gone a little over halfway, Matt heard faint voices up ahead and stopped in his tracks. Looking around, he found a boulder off the trail that would hide them from view if they could get to it quick enough.

"There," he barely whispered.

Becky nodded. To his surprise, her steps were light and nearly silent, despite the dead foliage that blanketed the forest floor. They both dropped low to the ground and waited. As the voices neared, Matt's pulse calmed and his heart sank in his chest. One of the voices obviously belonged to a female. He glanced at Becky and saw the same disappointment on her face.

"They looked creepy to me, Zach. Seriously," the girl was saying. "Can't you move any faster? They'll be right on top of us in two minutes at this rate."

"You're so judgmental, Alice," the guy grumbled. "They're probably really nice guys who felt threatened by that flag on your shirt."

"I swear. My dad was so right about you," she griped. "You have zero situational awareness. Those were not nice guys. And if they feel threatened by the American flag, why would they come here?"

"Your dad is closed-minded and prejudiced." Zach sounded like a complete beta. "He's indoctrinated you with his nationalist ideology."

"And?" Alice scoffed. "What's so wrong with loving our own country and believing that we should prioritize our values—which you enjoy the benefits of every day, by the way—over the ones that clearly aren't working out in the Middle East?"

"I am not having this argument with you right now."

"Because you don't have a leg to stand on," Alice shot back. "I thought college was supposed to make you smarter. What exactly are you paying them for?"

"All I know is—those men are going to think Americans are rude." Zach sounded like he might cry.

"So what?" Alice retorted. The couple was just on the other side of the boulder. "That one guy was rude to me. And everyone is indoctrinated by some sort of ideology. I'd rather be paranoid like my dad than trying to hold hands with creepers who talk to women like the one guy talked to me."

"You don't even know what he said!" Zach whined.

"Oh, but it's the way he said it." Their voices started to fade. "Like he was angry at my existence."

"They always sound angry. It's the way they talk."

"You're thinking of Germans, Zach. Arabic or whatever is supposed to be poetic sounding."

"No. You're wrong," Zach persisted. "Chinese is poetic. Italian, French, and *German* are poetic . . ."

Becky tapped Matt's arm, meeting his eyes when he turned his head. "What do we do?"

"Sounds like the guys are headed back this way already." He took a breath, debating the options. "I think we should stay right here. Hopefully they're as talkative as Alice and Zach. Will you be able to understand what they're say—"

Becky's stomach growled loudly, and her hands flew to cover it, eyes going wide.

"Or maybe they'll be as vocal as your stomach."

One hand moved from her stomach to her mouth, and at first he thought she was going to puke again. She squeezed her eyes shut and pressed her back against the boulder. Her face steadily grew redder until tears started to stream from the corners of her eyes. Her stomach growled a second time, and it was all Matt could do not to burst out laughing when Becky started to slide to the ground, shaking with the laughter she held in.

"Do you need a protein bar or something?" Matt whispered, earning a hard kick to his leg. "A simple no would have been fine, Rebecca."

"Stop," she quietly gasped.

"Fine," he whispered. "Suffer in silence."

"I'm going to kill you if the terrorists don't," she hissed when she finally regained control, but the smile on her face and the way her brown eyes were shining at him told a different story. She liked him. Even if she refused to admit it.

"That's dark." He kept a straight face, narrowing his eyes and shaking his head in disapproval.

Her lips disappeared completely when she curled them in and took a half-hearted swing at him. He caught her fisted hand in his before she made contact with his chest.

"Wait your turn. The terrorists haven't had their opportunity to—"

Becky's other hand flew up to cover his mouth, and all humor vanished from her face. She slowly removed her hand and raised it to tap her ear with the index finger. Matt gave one nod in response and listened for any sound, but the only thing he heard was rushing water in the distance.

After a few seconds of near silence, deep voices sent an icy chill straight through his bones. He couldn't make out any words, but the furrow of Becky's brow, the way she tilted her ear up, and her eyes shifting back and forth, barely blinking, gave him hope that maybe she understood the gibberish. When the voices got closer, he tried to differentiate between them, but he couldn't tell how many there were, and he for sure didn't understand the language any more than that it was some form of Arabic. A flash of red-hot fury coursed through him with the knowledge that terrorists were only a few yards away—in his county. He fought the urge to dispatch them right on the trail and be done with it.

Dear Lord, please let Becky understand every word they're saying right now.

Matt agreed with almost everything Alice had said, but the one point he wasn't sure about was the language. Maybe Zach was right about that. Either they were arguing, or whatever dialect of Arabic they were speaking *was* the angriest-sounding language ever.

Finally the voices faded to nothing and the daylight began to fade too. They would be trekking at least the final quarter mile in the dark, especially if they wanted to avoid catching up to the terrorists before they got back to Highway 215. Becky shivered beside him, adding to the sense of urgency he felt to get her out of the woods and safely back to her cabin in Rosman.

"Let's move." He stood, offering his hand. When she took it, hers was ice cold. He shrugged out of his jacket and held it out to her.

"You'll freeze," she protested, shaking her head.

"You're already frozen." He pushed it gently into her torso. "I'll be fine, Chief."

"Thanks." She closed her eyes once her arms were in the sleeves and let out a little moan, teeth chattering. "It's like a sauna in here. You put off a lot of heat, don't you?"

"Hmm." He had to stop himself from laughing. "Did you just call me hot again?"

"In the literal sense." She turned and started toward the trail. "Like a space heater."

"So I'm handy," he pointed out.

"And seasonal." She snickered under her breath. "Not much use for you half the time."

"Very funny. Okay, what were those guys saying?" he asked quietly, keeping right on her heels.

"The good news is, they didn't mention us at all, so maybe they didn't see us the second time they passed the truck. They don't seem worried that anyone is onto them."

"So they were talking about their plan," Matt surmised.

"That's the bad news. More confirmation of what we already know, but little more. One of them was obviously the boss. Something was off about his accent . . ."

"How many guys were there?" Matt cut in.

Becky looked over her shoulder like the question surprised her. "Three, as far as I could tell. If the fourth guy was with them, he's introverted or mute. Anyway, two were exactly what I expected: Yemeni. And they were talking about 'the hospitals' and—"

"Hospitals," he interrupted. "Plural?"

"Yeah." She went on. "And transmitters and towers. But they didn't say anything about electromagnetic devices, so hopefully it's only crude explosives."

"They're going to bomb hospitals and comms," Matt theorized. "Probably cell towers."

"That tracks, I guess." She sounded doubtful. "It's still not as detrimental as our intel suggests. In what scenario is blowing up hospitals and cell towers going to kill millions?"

"It's not. Not up here. And not down in Rosman." Matt's frustration would hit an all-time high if they didn't find the missing piece of the puzzle soon. "The closest hospital is in Brevard, to the east of Rosman. If they're talking about hitting more than one, it'll be urgent care facilities and small local clinics unless they move even further away to neighboring counties. For maximum impact in the region, one of the hospitals has to be Mission—in Asheville."

"How many beds do you suppose that one is licensed for?"

"Can't be more than a thousand. Maybe eight hundred?" He kicked a small limb from the middle of the trail. "That's where people would be airlifted for trauma though."

"It's all too small-scale." Becky flapped her arms, clearly as frustrated as Matt.

"Regardless—"

"It won't come to that." She finished his sentence. "We'll neutralize them tomorrow. They haven't finished making the bombs. One of the guys said they wouldn't be ready to place 'the rest' of them until Christmas Eve or early Christmas morning, and the guy who's totally throwing me for a loop wasn't happy about how close they were cutting it."

"So it still sounds like they're attacking on Christmas?"

"I think so." Becky's head bobbed in front of him. "Only what did he mean by 'the rest of them'?"

"You think they'll hit something early?" Matt moved to walk beside her for a few steps where the trail widened.

"Maybe. I think we need to put surveillance on them tonight and around the clock until we move in." She slowed, sidestepping a dry rotted log and bumping into Matt. "I'd have said that anyway, but I have the uneasy feeling that something is going down sooner than we've anticipated."

"And what's throwing you off about the boss?"

"He called them fools or idiots, something hateful . . . but he said that part in Pashto. Unmistakably. Which actually makes sense with how his accent was throwing me off."

"Pashto. So he's Afghan?" That made Matt's hair stand on end.

"Or Pakistani. Or maybe Iranian." She huffed, her warm breath visible in the dimming light. "I wish I recognized the inflections well enough to pick it up with what little he said, but it's not my strong suit."

"Hey." Matt tugged on her elbow, drawing them to a halt. "You understood the language. It doesn't really matter where he's from. You did great."

"It might." She bit down on her lip, which he could have sworn quivered right before her teeth sank into it, and her brown eyes glistened slightly. "It really might matter. We don't know what any variable means at this point."

"Okay." Matt grabbed both her shoulders and nodded. "But we know a heck of a lot more than we did a few hours ago. We're on the right track. We're going to take them down no matter what circle of hell they crawled out of to get here."

"I still don't understand why they'd be on this trail." Becky shook her head. "That's another variable. They were on mission, talking shop . . . which they could have done at the house, especially if the boss is stressed about their deadline. This trail has something to do with their plan. Is there a cell tower along the route?"

"Not that I know of, and if there is, it doesn't work worth a flip anyway." Matt let his hands drop to his sides and nodded to the trail ahead. "We need to get moving or we'll be in the dark for way too long."

"We definitely have to take one of them alive and find out what they're planning for Crystal Falls." Becky nearly stumbled on a root.

"Courthouse Falls," Matt corrected. "Crystal Falls is in Yellowstone."

"I actually knew that." She waved her right hand in the air. "I went with my parents when I was thirteen. I'm thoroughly disappointed that I didn't get to see this one. I love waterfalls."

"You'll have to stay a few days after we wrap this up." He grinned at the back of her head. "I'll take you to every waterfall in Transylvania County if you'll let me. That can be our fifth date."

She actually snorted a laugh. "You're really counting this as date number two?"

"Yep." Warmth spread across his chest when she didn't call him out for flirting.

"So what are three and four, Sunshine?"

"Lunch with Granny seems like a third date activity for sure," he mused. "And the op is obviously a date."

"Ugh. Your Neanderthal is showing again." She shook her head.

Matt reached up to grab hold of her arm. "Becky, stop."

"What is it?" She instantly tensed, hand going under her shirt to where he assumed her Glock was hiding.

"Look up," he whispered. "There's . . . mistletoe."

"Are you out of your freaking mind?" She whirled around, smacking him hard on the chest. "You're not funny. And I'm not falling for that. Never in a million years would I fall for that."

"I'm completely serious." He couldn't decide if he should laugh or tell her to forget he'd mentioned the parasite.

As if she couldn't help herself, she glanced up. With a double take, her eyes bulged and she looked back at him. "That's mistletoe."

"I told you so."

"I'm not going to kiss you . . . but I can't believe there's really mistletoe."

"You're trampling all over tradition, and you don't know what you're missing. I'll give you until the end of date number four, but I can't promise to be a gentleman after that. Adrenaline and victory are a powerful cocktail."

She made a poor attempt to hide her smile and started moving forward again. "If ops count as dates, I've had more boyfriends than Drew Barrymore."

"Should I understand that reference?"

"You're the romcom enthusiast. So yeah, you should."

"Ummm . . . I've got nothin'." He shrugged even though she wasn't looking at him.

"She has like thirty exes." Becky made a gagging sound. "Not exactly wholesome."

"I was blissfully unaware until now." He gaped at the back of her head.

"Sorry," she called over her shoulder.

Matt stayed as close as he could without stepping on her heels. "How am I ever going to enjoy *50 First Dates* or *Blended* again?"

"I'm sure you'll survive. There are plenty more ridiculous love stories for you to swoon over and try to act out in real life." The evil little laugh that came from her was the final straw.

"Careful, Becky," he leaned to whisper in her ear. "I'm also a big fan of thrillers, and it's getting dark."

"Oh, jeez. Shaking in my boots," she said sarcastically. "Nope. Wait." She licked her finger and held it up in the air. "There was a breeze. I'm good now."

He was about to demand she return his jacket when she tripped and nearly face-planted, throwing her hands out in front of her at the last second.

"Crap." Matt reached for her, but she was already pushing herself back up. "Are you okay?"

"Yeah, just a little muddy." She turned her palms up and gasped.

"You're bleeding." He knelt down to get a closer look at where the blood was coming from.

"No." She shook her head. "No, it's not my blood."

Her eyes snapped up to his, real terror flashing there.

"You don't think—" Becky swallowed the rest of her question when a faint pained cry sounded off the trail.

"Get your Glock," Matt instructed, his service weapon already in his hand. "And stay right on my six, head on a swivel."

The closer they got to the rustling of someone struggling to hold on to life, the more blood covered the ground. When the noises stopped altogether, Matt picked up his pace, following the trail of blood. Just when he was preparing himself for something horrific, the body came into view. It lay completely still.

Matt stopped a few feet away, Becky bumping into him. She seemed to bury her face in his back for a moment before she sucked in a breath and spoke.

"Who is it?" She sounded on the verge of tears. "Is it Alice or Zach? Or both? Oh, how would we know? We didn't even look at them."

He opened his mouth to reply, but Becky kept spiraling.

"Do you see a flag? If it's a woman with a flag on her shirt—"

Matt cleared his throat. "Becky," he said calmly, stepping aside and returning his gun to the holster.

She had her eyes squeezed tightly shut, which wasn't ideal for someone gripping a handgun.

"There's no danger now." He slid his hand over hers, taking the Glock when she released it.

"I can't look, Matt. There was no gunshot; they must have been stabbed."

When real alligator tears started to roll down her tan cheeks, he tucked the Glock under his arm and took her face in his hands, shushing her.

"Look at me, Becky," he whispered. "It's not Alice *or* Zach."

Her eyes fluttered open, still overflowing as she gripped his wrists, smearing blood on them. "How can you know that for sure?"

"Because I think his name was Bambi."

Chapter 8

SUNDAY MORNING, DECEMBER 22ND

ROB AND A HANDFUL of higher ranking task force members trickled into HQ around nine o'clock, three full hours after Matt, Conor, and Becky started the morning strategizing with the team of operators. Aside from the FBI agents monitoring the driveway that led to the terrorists' hideout, no one else was really serving a purpose, making Becky wonder why they'd bothered popping in at all. It was for show, to be able to stamp their name on the operation after the fact—assuming things went well.

"We've got them." Rob stuck his chest out, clearly proud of himself. "Positive IDs on all four Yemeni nationals that were caught on video surveillance at three separate supply stores. I've looked over the footage myself."

"What do you mean, they're all Yemeni nationals? That doesn't add up." Becky pored over the pictures Rob slapped down on the table in front of her. There was the passenger she'd seen right after throwing up on the side of the highway and three more men with similar features.

"Of course it adds up," Rob argued. "The plans were found in Yemen, weren't they? Since when are we assuming these guys *aren't* Yemeni?"

"Since I heard them speaking last night, which you would know if you hadn't gone back to your hotel early."

Rob crossed his arms, scowling. "I left when everyone else did, and I read your speculations in the email you sent."

She refused to take the bait.

"One of them is not a Yemeni national. There must be more than four of them in all." Becky inched out of the way when Matt and Conor joined them at the table to study the faces of the men in the photographs.

"Maybe you heard wrong or the guy has a lisp." Rob voiced his doubt, making it really hard to refrain from antagonizing him right back. "Or maybe not. What does it matter?"

"It matters. Possibly more than anything else." She shook her head in disbelief. Was he really that obtuse? "And I didn't hear wrong. It's literally my job to know the difference between Semitic languages and dialects. And being good at my job is how the guys with guns know who is friend and who is foe."

"But all four of *these* guys are enemies." Rob threw his hands up dramatically. "If there are more in the house, we'll get them too."

"You're missing the point." She jabbed a finger at the photos. "What if the man I heard isn't in the house when we send our guys in? Right now, we're looking at an incomplete list of enemies."

"Maybe. That's a big maybe." Rob pinned her down with a hard stare. "You're obsessing about the wrong details."

"I'm equally focused on all of them." She took a deep breath, evening out her tone as best she could. "Tunnel vision makes for a sloppy mission. Poor execution on the ground costs lives. We have to keep a bird's-eye view."

Loud chatter came over the FBI comms, drawing all of their attention when Rob's team near Balsam Grove alerted them to movement from the driveway. It wasn't the Tahoe, but an unmarked van pulled onto the highway heading south toward Rosman.

Becky met Matt's eyes, asking in a whisper, "Could that be Penny?"

"Negative. She has a small gray Honda, but I'm not sure the thing actually runs anymore."

"How does she get . . . the necessities?" Becky listened to the comms with one ear and Matt with the other, pulse ticking up when the second team south of the driveway confirmed the van appeared to have one male driver and no visible passengers and all of the windows were blacked out except for the three in front.

"Whit checks on her periodically." Matt pursed his lips, looking guilty. "My job isn't all that irks my cousin. She thinks I should put more effort into fixing what's broken. She doesn't understand." He shook his head. "I tried, Becky. Over and over, I tried."

"I believe you."

Becky snapped her head toward Rob when he sent an order for his guys to report when they reached the Rosman Highway.

"You'll fall back at that point, turn in the opposite direction of wherever the van goes. A two-man tac team will take it from there."

"What are you doing?" Becky stomped across the room, snatching the radio out of Rob's hand. All thought of civility flew out of her head as her blood pressure shot up like a geyser.

"The van is obviously loaded down with explosives." Rob's face reddened as he glared at her.

"You're clairvoyant now, are you?" Becky tried and failed to keep her voice calm. Jesus was probably shaking his head at her lack of self-control.

Rob squared his shoulders. "I'm sending in the EOD Marine and one of the Rangers. It makes the most sense."

Sanchez—the famed MacGyver of taking apart bombs—moved closer to them, determination on his face.

"You have no authority to do that." Becky gaped at Rob, holding the radio out of reach when he tried to take it from her hand. "We have no idea where that van is headed, and we need Sanchez on the actual op. The probability of explosives is way higher in the house than in that van."

"I'm not sending my guys on a suicide mission," Rob argued. "You can postpone the raid on the house. That van is moving right now to God-only-knows where. Weren't you the one talking about the big picture? What about the civilians that terrorist is about to blow up?"

Becky hated that he had a valid point. She gritted her teeth and took a deep breath. "You're right."

"I'm—what?" Rob was shocked into silence.

"You're right." She slammed the radio back into his hand. "But so am I. It wasn't your call to make. Send out one more order like that without clearance and I'll have Sheriff Woodhouse put you in a cell."

"You—"

"Stand down, Simms," Conor barked.

Becky didn't wait to hear the argument between Rob and Conor, stepping away and waving to the Raider and Ranger she had to deploy within the next five minutes.

Matt tapped his thigh repeatedly where he sat at the back of the makeshift HQ, agitation and anxiety building up in his mind, making his thoughts race faster than an F-15 Eagle fighter jet.

"I've been thinking." Becky settled beside him, bringing a delicious vanilla scent with her that made him crave Granny's sugar cookies.

"You too?" He rolled his head to the side, meeting her warm brown eyes. What he wouldn't give to go back to the simplicity of bantering about coffee and a budding romance.

Like the majority of the people in the room, she'd abandoned the formality of slacks. Her sensible pair of jeans, long-sleeved t-shirt, and ball cap made him think of the first day they'd met. If she hadn't introduced herself as a petty officer in Somalia, he might not have even realized she was in the Navy. The ponytail that protruded from her ball cap now was longer than the one she'd had back in the day.

"If Penny shows up at your granny's house, we can figure out how to keep her there, right?"

"Maybe." He swallowed the lump in his throat.

"But if she doesn't leave her house at all . . ."

Matt sighed, waiting for her to complete her sentence.

"Whit may be our only other option."

He already knew where Becky's thoughts had led her, because he'd gone there and back again three times. "I can't send Whit down that driveway, Becky. It's too risky."

"Hear me out." Her hand landed on his forearm. "I don't think we should *send* her in."

"You want me to go with her."

"Both of us," she rushed to say. "I'll go too."

"It's bad enough having Penny so near a ticking time bomb and considering risking Whit's safety on top of it." He crossed his arms. "I'm not letting you put yourself in danger for my mother too."

"First of all, you 'letting' me do anything is laughable."

"Your feminist is showing," he mumbled, earning him a backhand to the shoulder.

"Second of all . . . there isn't a second of all. That's really all I've got."

"If we go this route, I'm not asking Whit to walk into a hotbed of terror activity without telling her exactly what she's doing."

"Agreed." Becky didn't hesitate. "And I think we should loop her in regardless. If Penny does show up to Granny's house, we'll probably need Whit to understand how imperative it is to keep her there."

"She might laugh in our faces and hightail it out of town," he warned, trying to ignore the familiar way Becky talked about his cousin and grandmother and how it made his insides warm and fuzzy.

"Doubt it." Becky shook her head. "Whit didn't strike me as the type to tuck tail and run. And if she's the one who's been pushing you to reconcile and who's been taking supplies to your mom, she cares about both of you."

"You're annoyingly observant." He sighed. "Have I told you that?"

"Not in so many words." She leaned forward, aiming a sad smile up at him. "Since when are you the surly one, Sunshine?"

He let out a singular lazy "Ha" in response, annoyed that he couldn't actually enjoy her quip.

"So are we going to attempt this or what?" Becky prodded.

"Only one way to find out." He stood and offered his hand. "First we see if Penny shows up to lunch, which could go really poorly, by the way. You realize what this means, right?"

"I'm gonna meet Granny." She looked genuinely pleased with the prospect. "I promise to be sweet."

"You sure you wanna leave this place in Rob's hands?" He raised both eyebrows, knowing she'd been anxiously listening to the periodic reports from the guys following the van.

"We'll have a radio, and Conor assured me he's keeping Rob on a short leash." She chewed on her lip. "Where do you think the van is headed?"

"Raleigh." He didn't have a doubt. At first, when the van didn't stop at the nearest hospital, it looked like the driver was going to Asheville, but then he kept on driving. When he bypassed Charlotte five minutes ago, the air in the room grew thick with angst.

"That's what I think too. It makes sense, hitting the capital, but then . . . part of my brain is asking why they'd start making sense now." She glanced toward the group of FBI agents monitoring the comms. "It's a diversion. A bombing in the capital of North Carolina will cause every eye to turn in that direction for long enough to distract from the real attack."

"Probably." He nodded. "But they don't know that we're on to them. And the attack on Raleigh won't work. Sanchez knows what he's doing, right? He's got this."

"Yeah. You're right."

"I usually am." He grinned down at her, enjoying the glare he felt coming from Rob.

Chapter 9

12:30 P.M. - BALSAM GROVE

BECKY'S STOMACH WAS CRAMPED with discomfort. Whether the pain resulted from the stress of driving up Parkway Road, abandoning her post at HQ, or meeting more of Matt's family, she wasn't sure. At least she hadn't puked on the way up the mountain this time.

As they passed the dreaded driveway and the site where FBI agents were posted, Matt used the radio to alert the team that it was his tan Toyota Tacoma carrying them toward Balsam Grove. They drove on for a few miles before turning off to the left, passing what looked like an old fish hatchery and finally stopping in front of a structure that may once have been a barn but was clearly "Granny's House," as stated by the sign hanging over the front door.

Chipped red paint covered the tattered boards of the house, and children darted in and out of a side door that Becky could barely make out from where they parked. Inflatable Christmas decorations seemed to be the reason for the kids playing outside in the cold. As she gazed around the yard and fields beyond, cluttered with rusty farm equipment, barbed wire fences, and sloping hills that seemed to go on and on, delicate snowflakes began to drift down all around them.

Matt cleared his throat softly, breaking the spell that had her almost believing the world wasn't such a scary, broken place and that maybe she'd enjoy living at a slower pace on a homestead off the grid. A smile tugged at the corners of Matt's mouth when she turned to look at him.

"This isn't exactly how I wanted to introduce my girlfriend to my family."

"You're not really going to introduce me as your girlfriend, are you?"

She gulped, half hoping he *would* do it and not knowing where the insane desire stemmed from. Something was seriously wrong with both of them. She hadn't been able to stop fixating on the moment in the woods when she nearly suffocated holding her laughter at bay while the man who should have been telling her to calm down egged her on instead. How mentally unstable did two people have to be to find anything humorous while hiding from terrorists in the middle of remote woods? She should have been terrified at that moment, but she hadn't been.

Being next to Matt was easy. She felt safe with him, and she loved how often he made her laugh. Of course, tripping into a pool of blood and momentarily believing someone had been murdered right under their noses was a bit of a wake-up call in the end. Thank God it had only been a whitetail deer.

"What if I do?" Matt dropped the joking tone from his voice and studied her face so intently, her mouth went dry.

"You'd be lying to them, Matt." She glanced at the front door of the house, spying Whit with a broad grin on her face staring out at the truck and turning to talk to someone else inside before the door shut again. "I don't want you to lie, but I can't deny that it would make my presence less conspicuous and sure wouldn't hurt the security of our mission."

"Forget about OPSEC for a minute." His hand landed next to hers on the bench seat, not making contact but close enough that she felt the heat that radiated off of him. "You said it yourself—I've already invented our whole whirlwind romance in my mind."

"I did say that." Becky pursed her lips, warmth blooming in her cheeks.

"And my crazy little tropes aren't entirely off base, are they?"

"Perhaps not." She held her breath, looking at his lips for the tiniest millisecond—which, of course, made them twitch upward with that self-assured grin that seemed annoying only yesterday.

He leaned toward her ever so slightly, his thumb making contact with her pinky. "So perhaps it doesn't have to be a lie."

"Are you asking me to be your girlfriend, Matt?" Somehow they'd gotten close enough that she could smell the remnants of the candy cane he'd crunched on the drive up the mountain. What if his lips tasted as good as they smelled?

Just when Becky thought she might lean an inch closer, the FBI comms blared, obliterating the moment entirely.

She pressed her back into the passenger seat, willing her pulse to calm and listened to the back and forth between HQ and the surveillance team. Matt's wide eyes flashed to hers when the words "one female, red hair, driving a gray Honda Civic" rang out.

Matt gripped the radio, waiting for Rob to finish instructing a team to follow the Honda.

"HQ, this is Taylor. There's no need to tail the Honda. She's local, lives in the other house down that drive, and she can only be headed to one of two places."

"Can she? Do enlighten us, Taylor." Rob's voice grated on Becky, effectively murdering the butterflies that had been making laps around her stomach. She was ready to let go of her animosity toward Rob—she could already mark significant progress—but it would be easier to forget all about him when he wasn't actively being rude to people around her.

"She's either headed to her mother-in-law's house or the volunteer fire department." Matt waited for a reply. The delay seemed to go on forever.

"How do you know this . . . Pennilyn Anders . . . won't bring supplies back to her new neighbors?" an unfamiliar voice chimed in. "Correction, her tenants."

Matt growled before responding.

"The house rental is handled by an online third party. The terrorists probably don't even know she owns the house. And she doesn't speak to strangers. She hardly speaks to the few friends and family she has left." Matt took a deep breath and closed his eyes. "It's the Sunday before Christmas, so they'll have a care package of food for her at the fire department. And her family is already gathered for lunch."

"You know her family's every move too?" Rob again. "How convenient."

Becky reached her hand to Matt's shoulder. "You don't have to tell him anything, Matt. Let him waste his time and resources."

The radio was back to his lips before she finished speaking.

"I know . . . because I'm her son." Matt looked in the rearview mirror with a grimace. "And you can tell your guy in the SUV to keep driving past where she pulled off the highway, because I'm looking right at her."

Matt tossed the radio to the floorboard and scrubbed his hands over his face. "Becky . . . you need to know that she's probably going to say something horrible to you."

"I'll be fine," she assured him, suddenly more nauseated from how stuffy the truck had become.

"No, I mean—" He took a deep breath, knee bouncing up and down. "This was a bad idea."

"Changed your mind about our budding relationship already?" Becky sucked in a breath when a woman with a messy red bun walked right by the driver's side window.

Penny hesitated on Granny's small porch, petting Whit's mangy-looking dog before she knocked on the front door. Whit opened it, face blanching and eyes darting from Penny to Matt's truck. She quickly recovered and hugged the woman, ushering her inside. Whit paused on the threshold, widening her eyes at Matt and jerking her head toward the inside, mouthing, "What are you waiting for?"

"Can't we leave here and storm the house full of bad guys right now?" Matt asked, eyes fixed on Granny's front door.

"Matt, we're going inside Granny's house."

"This is more terrifying than any op. She hates me." He reached for Becky's hand, surprising her when he gripped it hard and looked her in the eyes. "But I'll slay any dragon you ask me to if you really will be my girlfriend."

"You charmer." Becky pulled her hand away, then shoved his shoulder and turned to open the passenger door. "Focus, Taylor."

Not the reaction I was hoping for.

Matt got out of his truck and met Becky at the front of it, reclaiming her hand, determined to present her as his girlfriend whether she confirmed it or not. The way she looked at him before Rob and his goons destroyed the vibe was all the encouragement he needed to stop playing around and start really pursuing her.

He wouldn't let this mission end with regrets and what-ifs. He'd put all his cards—and his bleeding heart—on the table and leave no doubt as to his sincerity. His mind was made up.

When he lifted his free hand to knock on Granny's door, Becky laced their fingers firmly together, stood on her tiptoes, and leaned close to his ear to whisper, "You being my boyfriend wouldn't be the worst thing in the world, I suppose."

His mouth fell open at the same moment Whit appeared in the doorway.

"Took you long enough," she muttered, standing aside for them to enter.

Granny's house was the same as always, full of boisterous conversations and children laughing. Only this gathering had the added noise of *The Christmas Story* playing on the television and the extra festive glow of Granny's oversized Christmas tree. The mouth-watering aromas of various meats, mashed potatoes, and an array of carb-loaded casseroles made his stomach growl and his memories run wild. The colorful dessert table looked exactly like it had every Christmas of his childhood, right down to the serving platters that Granny swore dated back to before the Civil War.

His grandmother smiled with a glint in her green eyes. Her snow-white hair seemed brighter than usual with the red and green dress she must've worn to church. It was a little jarring, considering Granny's usual style more closely resembled Whit's outdoorsy clothing choices.

Penny wouldn't look at him with more than a darted side-eye glare. And the rest of his large extended family had eyebrows raised in anticipation. Becky squeezed his hand, reminding him that she held it and alerting him to the silence that had fallen on the room.

"Hey guys, this is Rebecca Salazar—Becky—my girlfriend."

Penny grunted while most everyone else called out various welcomes and went back to their merriment. Granny shimmied to the edge of her seat, then stood with a little help from Whit. Matt tugged Becky forward, meeting Granny a few steps from her chair.

"Let me get a look at the two of you." Granny's mischievous smile played across her face. The sweet smell of spiced cider wafted off of her, comforting him. "As I expected, you've found the one, my boy."

A surprisingly pleasant sound came from Becky's throat, like a melodious little laugh mixing with a cough. One look at her face told him she was amused and maybe delighted by Granny's assessment. Had he hit his head? Was he dreaming or hallucinating?

"Just like his daddy, that one." Penny seemed to be talking to the Christmas tree, effectively murdering the delight that had built in his chest. "Likes 'em dark and foreign."

Matt tensed, but Becky reached up to squeeze his bicep. "It's okay."

Then she stretched out her hand toward Granny, saying, "It's so nice to meet you—" Her mouth gaped and her cheeks flushed. "I'm so sorry. Matt and Whit have only called you Granny."

Granny snatched Becky's hand and pulled her close, nearly causing Matt to lose his grip on her other hand, which had started to feel like a lifeline he desperately needed.

"And that's exactly what you can call me, sweetie. All my favorite people call me Granny." She gestured around the house. "Honestly, I don't think half these hooligans know the name my mother gave me."

"Good strong Appalachian name is what," Penny spat over her shoulder, having fully turned her back on them to look out the living room window. "Jeannie. Nice American name."

"Actually, Pen . . ." Granny eased back into her chair, turning the television off so that the room grew quiet enough for Matt to hear his own heartbeat throbbing in his ears. "Jeannie is French. Means God's grace."

Penny sat rigid, twisted unnaturally in the chair that belonged at the dining room table. She didn't respond, so Granny went on.

"Becky, you'll have to excuse my daughter-in-law. She's unfamiliar with the concept of grace." Granny tapped her chin thoughtfully. "Rebecca, you say? That's a good Bible name. Do you serve the Lord, Rebecca?"

Matt swallowed hard. He hadn't thought to prepare Becky for Granny's questions. He held his breath, knowing how much the answer meant to Granny—and how much it should matter to him.

"Yes, ma'am. Since I was eight years old." Becky inched closer to Matt's side.

"Mercy sakes. Where are our manners? Whit, let these two sit on the loveseat." Granny waved her hand. "Matthew Taylor, go get Whit a chair from the dining room and hurry back."

"Horrible name. Wretched name." Penny sneered toward him, still not meeting his eyes. He took a deep breath and let go of Becky, slumping away to obey Granny's instruction.

By the time he got back, Becky was in tears from laughing and Whit was contorted on the floor, describing what he could only guess was a dramatic mishap on a fishing trip. Granny shook her head in disapproval, and Penny had the slightest of smiles on her face—which disappeared as soon as she saw Matt. She jerked back around to face the window again, shoulders tensing.

"That's enough of that, Whit. Show a bit of decorum." Granny gave a singular nod and smiled at Becky when Matt joined her on the loveseat. "Now, tell me how the two of you met, and then we'll get some food."

Penny shook her head, hands fisting under her chin like a toddler.

"That's classified, Granny," Matt said apologetically.

"Only parts of it." Becky slapped his arm playfully. "The first time we met was six years ago, but it was very brief."

"I knew he left me for the same sort." Penny stomped her foot on the floor. "Just like his daddy. Just like his daddy."

"That's enough, Pennilyn," Granny said firmly. "If you'd like to join the conversation, you're more than welcome, but leave your venom out of it."

"You told me he wouldn't be here, Jeannie!" Penny snapped at Granny. "Promised it."

"I told you my son wouldn't be here," Granny shot back. "Like he hasn't been here the last twenty-two Christmases. But you knew Matthew might come."

"Doesn't usually." Penny shook her head vigorously, then seemed to get her thoughts jumbled. "Didn't show up any of those years he was with her. And here she is. Right in my face again."

"She's confusing you for someone else, Becky." Granny sighed sadly. "It's got nothing to do with you or Matthew."

"I know." Becky slid her hand back into Matt's. "I won't take offense."

Granny gave a grateful smile, then clapped her hands together. "Six years ago, you say? He was deployed that year to . . . nobody knows where. You must've caught him before he left the country."

"Um, no, ma'am." Becky's fingers tightened around his. Was she nervous too? "We met overseas."

"Ahh." Granny sat forward. "Then you can tell me where he was. You were in the Marine Corps too?"

"Certainly not." Becky chuckled. "I'm in the Navy. We . . . worked together for a day."

"Worked together where?" Granny lifted her chin.

"Ummmm." Becky hesitated.

"You're not going to tell me." Granny grimaced. "Tightlipped nonsense, if you ask me. The least you young folks could do is tell an old lady a good story now and again. Even if it's only the bit about you meeting."

Becky bit back a smile when Matt looked at her. He could see in her eyes that she wanted to appease Granny's curiosity.

"It's your call, Chief. It was your mission."

"Okay, then." Becky rubbed her free hand on her jeans nervously. "As far as our interaction, he brought me a cup of coffee, which was his lame attempt at hitting on me. As if I didn't know where the coffee pot was—sitting at the back of the room."

"Ow." He grabbed his chest. "You don't have to tell it like that."

"I'm only kidding. It was very sweet." She looked at Granny. "The gesture. Not the drink. Though he does make a delicious cup of coffee."

"Much better." Matt let his shoulders relax some.

"I'm the one talking here, Taylor." She held his gaze until Granny forced a cough.

"You were going to elaborate, I'm sure of it," Granny prodded.

After a second, Becky flinched ever so slightly, like someone had pinched her.

"That's really all there was to our face-to-face . . . but that day was special for another reason. I'm not sure Matt knows the specifics, actually."

He studied Becky's face, confused as to why her eyes were filled with tears. She cleared her throat and went on. "A lot of times, the guys like Matt—though they're the ones who actually go in and do the hard jobs—they don't know exactly why they're being sent to one location or another."

She was right. So many times he'd wondered about the targets they'd taken out on a given day, but before he could dwell too long on any one mission, he'd already been sent to another. That's how it went for almost the entirety of his career. He never doubted that the targets were a real threat, but that didn't mean he knew the specific evils they carried out to draw his crosshairs in their direction.

But Becky knew.

"My team works hard to build relationships and trust within the communities we are deployed to. More often than not, the bad guys we're looking for are the ones locals cross the street to avoid. It's not that the civilians necessarily want to help us, but . . . the enemy of my enemy is my friend, if you know what I mean."

Even Penny had her ear turned toward Becky at that point.

"In the weeks leading up to me meeting Matt and his cohorts, we had multiple reports of a particularly upsetting nature." Becky studied her hand clasped in his. "Without going into gratuitous detail, it wasn't safe for kids—young girls specifically—to go to school. The terrorists that had embedded themselves in the area went to extreme measures . . ." She sucked in a breath, wiping under her eyes with her free hand. "They, uh, made sure no parent would send their daughters to school anymore."

Becky looked back up, straightening her posture before she concluded, "That is, until Marine Raiders eradicated every last one of the terrorists in that cell."

Granny looked at Matt then, tears trickling onto her cheeks. "That's what you did, Matthew?"

He nodded, fighting his own emotions with all his might. "Yes, ma'am."

Penny met his eyes then. For a split second, he saw the woman who used to chase him through the house until he collapsed in a fit of laughter, who sang him to sleep every night and stayed with him during thunderstorms. Then as quickly as she'd appeared, she vanished behind the mask of confused bitterness and turned away again.

"I'll be," Granny whispered, looking at Becky. "You sure didn't hold out on me, sweetie. And it's no wonder the two of you found each other again. It's like I said, you're meant to be."

Granny pushed herself to stand. "Round everybody up and let's eat. You're saying grace, Matthew."

Chapter 10

"We've really got to talk to Whit. Penny is starting to pace." Becky looked Matt in the eyes when they'd cleaned up their lunch plates. Her prodding caused a grimace of discomfort and hesitation to fill his face. "If she leaves here . . ."

With a grunt, he turned toward his cousin, who was pouring cup after blessed cup of coffee in the kitchen. She automatically handed a steamy mug to Becky, then did a double take of the two of them hovering right beside her.

Becky moaned with delight as she sipped the beverage. "How is the coffee so good here?"

"It's the water," Whit responded, holding a cup out to Matt, who turned it down with a shake of his head. Whit shrugged, placing the coffee on the counter and glancing back at Becky. "Help yourself to some dessert, Becky. There's a month's worth, at least."

"No, I'm good with the coffee. What do you mean, it's the water?"

"Mountain water," Whit elaborated. "You won't find any better than it is right here."

Matt snorted. "Whit is passionate about her Carolina waterways."

"Oh, right. Because of the fishing." Becky nodded, glancing at Penny and trying to think of a good segue into the more important subject.

"Hey, these creeks and rivers are way more important than that," Whit chided Becky.

Matt sighed, leaning over to explain, "She has a doctorate in forest management. Literally. She could talk to you for hours about the importance of hugging trees. Zach would worship her."

"Laugh it up, Matthew Taylor. One day you'll see that being good stewards of the resources God gave us is no joking matter. When the whole world is imploding—"

"Siiiimmer dowwwn." Matt stretched his words out dramatically. "You know I'm only messing with you."

Becky nudged Matt with her elbow, mumbling, "Will you move this along?"

"Look, Whit, we actually need to talk to you in private."

"How'd I know the two of you didn't come here to spend quality time with family and celebrate the holiday?"

Whit turned on a dime, leading them into a hallway off the kitchen and past several doors until they were out of earshot. From where they'd parked outside, the cute farmhouse looked smaller and deceptively shabby. Everything inside was updated, from the hardwood flooring to the bright white shiplap on the walls. Staring down the hallway, Becky guessed it had at least five bedrooms. Did Granny live here all alone? The fly-fishing pictures and classically tacky Christmas décor seemed to suggest Whit had a hand in decorating.

"What is it now?" Whit demanded.

Matt opened his mouth to speak, but Whit cut him off before he could get a word out. Becky's eyes widened when Whit addressed her directly.

"Was that story real, Becky? This"—She gestured at the two of them—"Is this real? Because I was only messing with you, Matt, when I suggested you bring your 'lady friend.' Please tell me you'uns weren't puttin' on a show for Granny. That might work in the movies, but it's despicable to try it in real life."

"Every word I said was true, Whit." Becky slid her hand into the crook of Matt's elbow. "And maybe we're still finding our footing, but I-I wanted to be here today. Like this."

"Ew." Whit flipped some internal switch, suddenly more appalled about the idea of Becky being with Matt than only pretending she was. She shoved blonde flyaway hairs out of her face and made a gagging sound. "Why? You could do so much better."

Matt let out a heavy sigh, shifting his weight. "Are ya done?"

"I reckon." Whit shrugged as if maybe she wasn't done and he should be ready for more ribbing in the near future.

"Penny is in danger." Becky blurted the words out. "Real danger. From the four guys you told us about yesterday."

"They're in the rental house." Matt picked up where Becky left off.

"Who are they?" Whit hissed, hazel eyes going wide.

"They're like the men from my story earlier." Becky was crossing a line, but like she'd told Matt earlier, Whit needed to understand the severity of the situation.

"They're terrorists?" Whit took a step backward, then set her coffee down on a slim table in the hallway. "I mean, the thought did cross my mind. But they're in Penny's rental? Right now?"

"Yes," Becky confirmed. "Penny can't go back home."

"Why aren't you arresting them?" Whit demanded of Matt.

"It's not that simple." He shook his head.

"How long until it's simplified?" Whit's lips barely moved as she seethed.

"Not today. Maybe by tomorrow morning." Becky was giving her way too much information, but it felt like they were backed against a wall. "Whit, can you keep Penny here?"

"It won't be easy." She shook her head and released a heavy sigh.

"You can't tell anyone else why," Matt informed her.

"I'll have to tell Granny," Whit argued in an alarmed whisper. "She's the only one that'll be able to convince Penny to stay."

Matt growled under his breath, looking defeated. He turned to Becky and said, "She's right."

"Fine," Becky conceded. "But *no one* else."

"Alright." Whit was nodding vigorously. "I've got it. There's one thing that might help get the ball rolling. Matt, you remember when we didn't want to come home from Lake Keowee that summer after Papaw died?"

"Way ahead of you." Matt slid his arm from Becky's grasp but caught her hand and planted a kiss on it before he walked further down the hall and out what she assumed was the side door she'd noticed when they first arrived.

"Where is he going?"

"To make sure Penny's car won't crank." Whit's lips pulled into a devious smile as she jerked her head toward a window. Becky followed her, catching sight of Matt as he ran across the yard, bypassing his truck and ducking down somewhere near Penny's Honda. After a minute of silently watching his blond hair pop in and out of view, Whit whispered, "The real trick will be convincing Penny not to walk home or hitch a ride. Granny should be able to handle it. I'll go talk to her in a minute."

"Can you tell me what exactly happened there? With Penny and Matt." Becky regretted the question as soon as she asked it. It wasn't any of her business.

Whit pushed off the wall, shoving her hands in her back pockets. "It's really not my place. You should ask Matt about it though."

"Should I?" Becky took a long drink of the coffee in her hand.

Whit eyed her for a few seconds before she slowly nodded. "Yeah. If you meant what you said about wanting to be with him."

"Okay." Becky took a deep breath, not knowing what else to say. Whit changed the subject before things got awkward.

"If Granny can't convince Penny to stay put . . ."

"We don't want to upset her." Becky looked over Whit's shoulder, where Matt had already slipped back into the house. "But we'll detain her if we have to. Better she be alive and traumatized by men in black suits than caught in a firefight or worse."

"You'll let me know when it's okay for her to leave?" Whit blew out a heavy breath when Matt stood at Becky's side again.

"Yeah." Matt looked down at Becky. "We should head back to Rosman. See what we've missed."

"Right." Becky drained her cup with one final gulp. Looking up at him, she added, "I get it now."

"Get what?" Matt took her empty cup, rudely shoving it into Whit's hands.

"The draw to Appalachia. The coffee alone is worth settling down here." She blushed when both of them raised their eyebrows. Replaying her words in her head, she realized how they could allude to future possibilities. Surprisingly, she was more tempted to explore the thought than to correct any misunderstanding. She simply said, "We'd better say bye to Granny."

When they'd settled into Matt's Tacoma and started down the mountain, he called in their location and alerted HQ of their ETA, informing them that they had the "Pennilyn Anders situation" handled for the time being and requesting an update on the van.

As they'd theorized, the driver had stopped at a motel south of Raleigh. He'd settled into a room at the motel, but no further word had been sent. The two-man team was supposed to report on the situation again in half an hour, so long as there was no movement beforehand, and then a decision would be made on how to proceed.

Becky took a nervous breath, dreading the probability that she'd have to ask Sanchez to defuse a bomb before he returned to Rosman to potentially defuse countless more. One of the hardest parts of her job was knowing that what she asked of brave men could cost them their lives in an instant.

God, please go before them. Before all of us.

"You okay?" Matt gently touched her elbow. "Let me know if we need to pull over."

"I think I've got my bearings now, as far as the curves on this road go." She looked out the passenger window. It wasn't snowing at the moment, but some of the earlier dusting had accumulated. It was different from the snow in Colorado. There, in the mountains west of Denver, everything had a sharpness to it. Appalachia was softer, slower-paced, and more peaceful than majestic—though it wasn't without breathtaking beauty all its own.

"I'm sorry about Penny." Matt's voice sounded small.

"Me too." Becky fought the urge to slide closer and lay her head on his shoulder. "I know that wasn't easy for you."

He only nodded, taking the curves with caution.

"What happened to her, Matt?" she asked softly. "I mean, bitterness, I understand—if your dad cheated, left her, and broke her heart. But what drove her mind away, or was she always like that?"

"She—she started to fade away little by little after Dad left. I was only six." He slowed to swerve around a branch that had fallen from a tree, obstructing half of the lane they were in. "The court ordered joint custody, so it's not like he fully left me or anything. It was hard at first, figuring out how to navigate that life when I didn't really understand what was happening."

"I can't imagine that." She closed her eyes, heart aching for the small boy caught in the middle of his parents' broken lives.

"As I got older, I lied a lot to my mom . . . to mitigate the pain. I wanted to be with Dad on his days, and I loved Rosa—my stepmom—but even if I didn't, it wasn't up to me to decide where I went on any given day." He licked his lips, voice getting heavier. "About halfway into middle school, Penny began seeing my time away at Dad's as a world-ending betrayal. All the hate she directed at Dad and Rosa in the first several years, she started to direct at me."

"Is that when you got the scar on your cheek?"

"Yeah. But . . . it's not like she actually beat me or anything. She would just randomly lose it and throw something across the house. Things would break, and I'd get hit with shards of glass. Maybe I'd try to hug her when I got home from school and she'd freak out trying to get away from me, causing me to fall into furniture. Stuff like that." His grip on the steering wheel seemed to tighten for a moment. "It got bad enough that Dad petitioned for full custody when I was in eighth grade."

"Did he get it?"

"Penny didn't bother showing up to court. Didn't try to fight it." Matt cleared his throat. "That's when her mind really went. I don't know if she was trying to hold on to her sanity all that time and then finally gave up, or if being alone drove her fully insane. Either way—"

"It's not your fault." Becky studied the side of his face, watching his jaw clench and unclench. "You have to know that."

"When I was seventeen, I tried really hard to fix things with her. I'd go to the house and mow the grass or repair stuff that had broken. Sometimes she'd come out and nod her head at me, then run back inside. Or she'd be lucid enough to say thanks as I was leaving," He took a deep breath. "One day toward the end of senior year, she came out as soon as I drove up, and it was like she wasn't crazy at all. She was talkative, hugged me, and asked me to come back and see her more often. I thought, 'This is it. Mom is back. It's going to be okay.' Then the next time I showed up, she was off her rocker. Worse than what you saw today . . ."

"I'm so sorry, Matt."

"I never went back after that. I left for boot camp a couple of months later, and I . . . never went back. I've run into her from time to time, but she either acts like she did today or like she doesn't know me at all."

"Would medication help her?"

"Probably." He shrugged. "Granny and Whit have tried to convince her to get help, but she doesn't think she needs it. She doesn't actually hurt anybody, and she takes care of herself well enough. There's never been any indication that she's on harmful substances, so everyone just lets her be."

They were nearing the end of Highway 215, coming up on Whit's store, which was closed for the day of rest. Matt pulled into the deserted parking lot at the last second, rolling to a stop. The radio fell to the floorboard, but Becky ignored it and kept her eyes on Matt's pained expression.

"Becky, I saw her today."

"Yeah . . ."

"Not Penny the crazy shut-in. I saw my *mom*. It was there in her eyes for a fleeting second. She was staring right at me." His face crumbled completely before he rubbed his hands over it. "The woman that loved me before life robbed both of us. I think maybe she's still in there. Ya know?"

Becky couldn't see if he was crying, not through her own blurry eyes. Neither of them spoke for a minute, during which snow began to fall again. It wasn't a whiteout, but it was heavy and lovely and seemed to calm both of them.

"It was your story that did it." Matt finally spoke again, voice more even.

"What do you mean?"

"When you talked about Somalia, that's when she looked at me. Just for a moment." He took a deep breath, staring straight ahead at the falling snow or the river beyond. "Thank you for going with me."

"Of course." She turned toward him, suddenly wishing he hadn't called in an ETA at all.

"You were right. I never knew why we were there, other than to neutralize a threat." He finally looked her way. "What did they do . . . to the school girls?"

Becky lifted her eyes to the ceiling and blew out a breath. She wasn't prepared for him to ask for more details, but something in her gut told her he needed to know. Maybe, like her, he'd doubted things about his past, whether he'd taken the right path or if he'd really made a difference.

Her lip quivered, stomach twisting painfully as she spoke the words. "Beheadings. Three of them." She lost control of her tear ducts and struggled to keep her breathing even. "Three beautiful, bright, loved little girls went to school one day and never came home. None of them were older than twelve. Their only offense . . . was learning to read."

Matt stared at her for a long second. "How do you do it?"

"My job?"

He nodded.

"The same way you do, I guess. One day at a time. Lots and lots of asking God why . . ." She shrugged. "But I'm so *tired*, Matt. I need a reprieve."

"What's stopping you?"

Wiping her tears away was useless—they kept falling as she thought about his question.

"Little girls in Somalia who want to go to school. Christians in Syria being persecuted for their faith. Small Appalachian towns that don't know they're in imminent danger." She tossed her hands up, feeling hopeless. "What if I stop and no one else sees them?"

Matt seemed to be considering his response carefully before he gave it.

"God sees, Becky. And it's God who gives you sight." His words pierced her heart. "He directs our paths. He sent us both to Somalia six years ago. He sent you here now. And maybe it's him telling you to take a step back and find rest."

"Yeah, but—"

"Don't make yourself more important than you really are," he said gently.

"Ouch." She blinked at him, soaking in the truth of his words and the conviction that came with them.

He grimaced. "I don't mean—"

"I know." Becky closed her eyes for moment, collecting her thoughts as a sharp pain shot through her chest. "And you're right. I think that's exactly what I needed to hear, even if it stings worse than a fattail scorpion."

His eyes widened as he said, "I'll have to take your word for it."

"Count your blessings."

After staring at each other for a moment, Becky spoke again.

"I didn't want to come here," she admitted. "I wrestled with God the entire way."

He chuckled as if it didn't surprise him. "You don't say."

"Shut up." She tried not to smile, but it was increasingly impossible around him.

"God wanted to give you a second chance to see we belong together, Becky." His green eyes twinkled. "Stop fighting his plan."

"Do you mean God's plan or yours?" She felt the last of her reservations slipping.

"They might be the same thing."

With a deep breath, she whispered, "I'm here, aren't I?"

"What exactly are you saying?" Matt tilted his head.

"Hey, you heard Granny with your own two ears." She leaned toward him, hoping he'd take a hint.

"Granny said we're meant to be. Like I said we're meant to be."

A shiver ran down her spine when his eyes roamed her face and his fingers slid under her palm where it rested on the seat. His thumb brushed back and forth on top of her hand. "But *you* said you weren't going to fall for me."

"I've been wrong before," she confessed. "It's rare, but it happens. We both know you've been making things up as you go—don't deny it. Granny, on the other hand . . ."

"Granny is never wrong." Matt shook his head ever so slightly.

"That's what I figured."

Maybe it was the snow falling all around or the sheer quiet that blanketed them, but in that moment, the whole outside world—the threats and responsibilities—faded away. All that existed was the cab of the Toyota and the green eyes fixed on her. For years, she'd stayed one step ahead of the lonely, empty feeling buried deep in her gut. For once, she didn't have the will to carry on, push forward, or dig deeper. She wanted to be still. She wanted to rest. And, dang it all, she wanted to kiss the lips off of Matthew Taylor like there was no tomorrow.

Gripping his hand, she leaned the rest of the way toward him and pressed her lips to his. She must've shocked him, because he sat back slightly and looked at her, dazed.

"Is that all it takes to render you speechless, Deputy Taylor?" Becky snickered, not backing down.

She witnessed the exact moment it dawned on him that he hadn't imagined the kiss. The warmth of his hand landed on the right side of her neck. His lips claimed hers, and oh buddy, they hit the spot. Somehow he unfastened her seatbelt and pulled her to the center of the cab in one swift motion. Becky's fingers slid into the blond hair she suddenly understood the use for. It was the perfect length to get just the right hold on.

They both got completely lost in the moment of mutual release, trading the pain and loneliness that few others could comprehend for a chance to share each other's burdens. Neither of them noticed the approaching figures until it was too late.

Chapter 11

A FIST BANGING ON the glass of Matt's driver's side window pulled him from the perfectly diabolical lips of Rebecca Salazar. He'd never recover. If the disapproving glower on Conor Flynn's face was an indication, he might not survive the consequences anyway. At least he'd die happy.

"Crap." Becky sounded as breathless as he was. She bent down to pick up the radio from the floorboard. "The battery fell out. No wonder it was so quiet."

"Found them. They're both fine." Conor's muted voice should have played through the comms in the truck, but there wasn't a peep. "Looks like engine trouble at the base of the mountain."

Becky scrambled back to the passenger side and opened the door at the same time Matt jumped out of the truck.

"Have the two of you completely cracked?" Conor demanded. His brother Declan stood back several feet, staring at the snow-covered gravel with a huge grin on his face. Conor practically yelled, "You missed your ETA, wouldn't answer comms, and all so you could—"

"Con." Declan lifted his hands in the air. "Give the guy a break."

"I swear, Declan." Conor looked like he might spontaneously combust. "Now is not the time."

"If not now, when?" Declan persisted. "We could all be dead by tomorrow."

"You're not helping." Conor shook his head aggressively back and forth. "Do you even grasp how utterly unhelpful you are?"

"Yeah. I'm a huge waste of space, right up until you're bleeding out, lost in the forest, or down by two guys for a mission."

"Down two guys?" Becky interjected, panic lacing her tone.

Conor ignored Declan completely then, turning back toward Becky.

"HQ is in an uproar. The two guys in Raleigh aren't coming back any time soon."

"What happened?" Becky gasped.

"They lost the van." Conor huffed. "A fluke accident blocked them from tailing the terrorist when he took off again."

"I thought the van was parked for the night." Matt clamped his mouth shut when Conor glared at him.

"So did we. Or so we hoped. Maybe the driver got hungry. Or maybe he's on his way to blow something up as we *stand here doing nothing helpful*!" Conor growled.

"Conor." Becky spoke calmly. "What do we need to be doing?"

"Heck, I don't know." He tossed his hands up, deflating. "Raleigh police have eyes on the motel in case he comes back, but if he doesn't, we may have a mass casualty event tonight, tomorrow, or God-only-knows when."

"And what are they saying at headquarters?" Becky questioned.

"The brass and pretty much everyone are antsy—especially with the two of you MIA. They want to move on with the op tonight without the guys in Raleigh. They gave the all-clear for Dec and Kael to step in." Conor gulped. "Kael knows a guy who was EOD before his medical discharge. We can't send him *in* exactly, but he'll be nearby and talking the team through anything that might arise. We've got a SWAT guy being briefed in now, but you know it's not the same as Sanchez. He eats Yemeni IEDs for breakfast."

Matt chanced a step in Conor's direction. "Should I be headed back up the mountain?"

"Not yet—there's still several hours of hurry up and wait." Conor didn't look at him.

"Exactly." Declan shook his head in exaggerated disapproval. "Why is it that we couldn't leave these two alone for a bit longer? There's still plenty of time—"

"There isn't time for *that*," Conor spat out. Finally looking at Matt, he said, "Once we jump your truck off, it's straight back to HQ for the both of you." He pointed between Matt and Becky. "Matter of fact, Becky is riding with me. You can take my idiot brother with you, Matthew. That way I won't kill him and you won't get lost at the ballfield or gas station or elementary school and cost Becky her career. Sound like a plan?"

"Roger. Only I don't need a jump." Matt grimaced when the red of Conor's face deepened to nearly match his hair.

"Ooohh, yes, you do. And you'll take it. And you'll like it. And you'll thank me for it."

"Um, yes sir." Matt cleared his throat and took a step back away from Conor, not entirely sure what jumping off a fully functioning truck battery may or may not do.

Matt was scared to look at Becky, even when Conor turned his back and stalked toward his black SUV. He only turned to her when she gripped his elbow.

"I'm so sorry," he whispered.

"Are you sorry you did it, or sorry you got caught?" The glint in her eye gave him hope that he hadn't completely screwed up his chances. "You do realize that I'm the one who kissed you first, right?"

"Right. And you , , . don't regret it?"

"Mmmm." Her head bobbed back and forth as she seemed to be debating it. "How about you don't get shot or blown up, and I'll let you know what I think when we do it again."

"Roger that, Chief." It was all he could do to keep his hands to himself.

She cleared her throat and stepped back when Conor pulled his SUV right up to the hood of the Tacoma, glaring at them through the windshield.

"For now, we'd better refocus our energy." Becky barely moved her lips as she spoke, probably so Conor couldn't read them.

"Right." Matt shoved his hands into his pockets. "I think that's for the best."

She winked at him as she moved to get into the passenger side of Conor's vehicle.

"Good work, Taylor." Declan stepped right up beside Matt when Conor came back into earshot, carrying jumper cables. "Kael can give you pointers on wifing a Latina if you want some."

"I appreciate that, Declan, and I beg your finest pardon, but please pipe down before Conor shoots one of us."

Becky cleared her throat, suffocating in the silence of Conor's SUV. He opened his mouth, then closed it again. After a few seconds, he finally said, "You gotta help me understand, Becky."

"You had to be there." She rubbed her temples, embarrassed and astounded with herself but still not sorry.

"Oh." Conor huffed with the word. "I was there. Believe me, I wish I hadn't been."

"It was—" Becky searched for the words. "The end of the line. For both of us, I think. We've both been running from something or toward something . . . maybe around it. I dunno, Conor. It's like we both stopped in the same place at the same time. I can't explain it."

"Clearly." He turned off the highway, heading into Rosman. "I mean, the stakes couldn't be higher, yet there you were . . . *necking*."

"Gross. Don't call it that." Becky gagged. "How old are you?"

"Old enough to know there's a time for necking and a time for . . . not necking."

"I'm gonna hurl."

"What's going on with you, really?" Conor's tone softened. "I know you, Becky. You're straight-laced, mission-minded, and laser-focused."

"Yeah, and that's all I am. That's all I have." She shifted in the seat, taking in the Christmas lights that were strung all around the blissfully unaware town. "Every day, I see and hear the most heinous things imaginable. The pressure to stay one step ahead of the enemy is . . . you know what that's like, Conor."

"I do."

"And since Rob, I've accepted that this job is my calling. My purpose. That I'm not meant to have a family or a normal life or someone to share it with in an intimate way."

"Wait—" Conor pulled up to Town Hall and looked over at her, but she went on. "What if I was wrong to believe that?"

"You were one hundred percent wrong to believe that." Conor nodded.

"Right?"

"But—" Conor looked thoroughly befuddled.

"No buts. I just happened to realize I was wrong about two minutes before you found us." She leaned forward slightly. "And you interrupted the first kiss I've had in three years."

Conor nodded, gulping. "I bet that was frustrating."

"Very. But we shouldn't have been irresponsible." She shook her head. "You were right to be angry."

"I concur."

"So we're on the same page." Becky clapped her hands together.

"Okay, but who is mad at whom *now*?" Conor asked.

"Why should anyone be mad?" She tilted her head, matching his confused expression. "I had an epiphany, Matt figured out he might actually have a chance at stealing my heart, and you saved the day by finding us and getting us safely back to HQ." She patted his forearm. "Now let's go take down some terrorists so I can get back to necking."

"Bleh." Conor cringed. "I see what you're saying about that sounding gross. Let's bury that word in a deep, dark hole."

"One more thing we agree on." Becky sighed contentedly as she exited the SUV.

She might be on her last mission or she might have another fifty years of chasing creeps ahead of her, but whichever way the tide was turning, she knew God was in control, and she wouldn't try to wrestle with that reality anymore. When Matt slapped her with the truth a few minutes ago, it had wounded her pride, to be sure. The more she let his words sink in, though, the more liberated she felt. She had tried to take the helm from God in her career. Had she done the same thing in her personal life? The answer was painfully obvious.

God, forgive me for getting things twisted. Give us all eyes to see, ears to hear, and solid ground to stand on. Your will be done in this mission . . . and every other area of my life.

ZERO-DARK-THIRTY MONDAY, DECEMBER 23RD

Matt took a deep breath, steadily trekking through woods that he knew like the back of his hand. The steps of the other six men in the vicinity were barely audible. Thankfully, the snow was only slightly icy. The green hue of night vision didn't belong in this place, where he'd carved his initials into trees, shot his first squirrel, and stepped on a rat snake when he was eight years old. He could still remember the terror of thinking he would die from the harmless bite.

It was Penny—*Mom*—who had knelt down to dispel his fears, calmly explaining, "That little guy was just as scared as you are now, Matty. Fear isn't always a bad thing. You scared him back to where he won't get crushed underfoot, and he taught you to watch where you're stepping."

Kael Flynn crouched down several yards in front of Matt, having reached the edge of a tree line that would be their cover until they were given the order to move in. Clearing a structure was second nature to all seven of the men after doing it countless times for years on end, but the thought of clearing this house made Matt's stomach bottom out.

He'd never asked Dad why he bothered to build Penny's dream home when he never planned to live in it with her. He didn't need to hear Dad confirm that it wasn't a labor of love but one of guilt—his last act of service for a woman he'd already decided to betray. She never moved into the house. It sat empty for years before Whit convinced Penny to at least use it to support herself. Matt wished he could understand his mother. Was it that she couldn't abandon the home that held the only good memories she had? She'd escaped an abusive father when she married Dad, believing in a forever that lasted less than seven years. Could she not stomach the thought of living in a home built by a man who promised to hold only her, then broke his vow?

Matt didn't know how to pray for her anymore. His petition had long since been simplified to "Help her, Lord."

Chatter on the radio broke through the heavy thoughts in Matt's brain, reminding him that there was a new breed of predator on this property, and like the rat snake had taught him, he needed to watch where he was stepping. He took a deep breath, seeing the dark silhouette of the Tahoe parked in the yard. It made him think of Alice and Zach on the trail to Courthouse Falls and how they'd come face to face with men who wouldn't think twice about killing them for the glory of a false god.

"Move in." Hearing the anticipated words set off a chain reaction of swift movement among the operators, all of them falling into their assigned positions at the front and back of the structure. Muscle memory took over Matt's body as they entered the house, methodically clearing it room by room. One terrorist was shot dead when he attempted to engage the operators who cleared the kitchen. The team moved swiftly, subduing not three but *eight* additional jihadists. There had been nine men in all, and Matt would bet anything that at least one of them was from somewhere other than Yemen.

When the call to initiate a back clear rang out from the furthest point of the house, Matt's adrenaline tapered off by a fraction. The call was repeated until the team had verified all threats were neutralized.

Along with Kael and a Ranger nicknamed Chester, Matt held the captured men at gunpoint while the FBI moved in on the location. Someone confirmed a cache of what appeared to be explosive devices stored in the old barn that sat between their current location and Penny's house. Matt shivered at the thought. That structure hadn't been stable when he was a kid, and it wasn't farfetched to imagine it caving in on the bombs and blowing the whole mountain sky high. According to the SWAT team asset and veteran EOD tech, they weren't in much danger, but Matt would feel a whole lot better when every ounce of ammonium nitrate was accounted for and unable to do anything more than make grass greener.

Becky's voice registered in Matt's ear, but not over the comms. She'd walked through the front door, and he swallowed the urge to demand she turn right back around. She was in her element, doing what she came here to do, and he had to breathe and bear it. The uneasy feeling that all of this had been too easy tugged at his subconscious, but he reminded himself that they'd had so many advantages over the terrorists, this outcome was inevitable. Not every mission had to have collateral. And there was still the matter of the van in Raleigh. No one but a complete lunatic would really call this ordeal "too easy."

"Do any of you speak English?" Becky questioned the room, obviously addressing the subdued men. No one so much as breathed heavy. Turning to Conor, she sighed loudly and said, "Find me an Arabic translator to meet us at the county jail as soon as possible."

"That could take a while." Conor played his part well.

"Just get it done," she snapped. "We need to understand why these guys were hiding in the middle of nowhere building bombs. They must have planned to transport them somewhere. Washington or New York."

Becky turned her back on Conor, holding up the pictures of the four men they'd already identified.

"I'm on it." Conor nodded at the back of Becky's head.

She waved a dismissive hand over her shoulder, earning a rehearsed glare from Conor before he left out the front door with his phone to his ear.

"You." Becky looked at Matt as if he were no more than a grunt in boots. Despite knowing this was part of the plan, it made his chest tight when she acted as if he were someone she could forget as easily as his own mother had. "Did you see this guy? Is he the dead one?"

"Negative. Haven't seen one quite that ugly." Matt looked at each man in turn. "He's not here."

"That's not good. Looks like we have a runner. Must've slipped by you guys."

Matt watched the faces of the terrorists. One close to the back pursed his lips, and two of them glanced at each other. They bought the charade—Matt could see it in their eyes. Becky called out an order to sweep the house for any identification, medications, and weapons, then to load the men up and move out to the county jail, where they'd be shown to their temporary accommodations.

"We Americans are nothing if not hospitable, after all." Becky settled into a chair several feet behind where the men were all bound and kneeling, facing away from her.

She shot a sly look directly at Matt. One of the terrorists hissed something to the man next to him, earning an elbow to the ribs.

"Don't move!" Matt pointed his rifle at the two men, who both nodded and looked at the floor.

A satisfied smile pulled at Becky's lips before she yawned and stretched, then winked at him. His heart fluttered in his chest. She really was good at what she did, having already set the terrorists up for failure. With each passing minute, they'd grow more sure that none of the infidels could understand them and more likely to talk amongst themselves. Whatever wasn't discovered in physical evidence, they might learn through the slipping of forked tongues.

Chapter 12

10:45 A.M. - ROSMAN

BY THE TIME THEY'D made it to the jail and put half of the terrorists into an intake room large enough to hold them all together, Becky had already learned that at least seven of the nine terrorists were from Yemen. They'd also talked about the driver of the van, calling him by name and confirming that he was in fact the same one who'd been seen buying fertilizer. The dead guy was another one the task force already identified through Rob's work with the local store owners. That meant that the man who hadn't uttered a word might be her Pashto-speaking ringleader. She couldn't rest easy on the assumption, but she held out hope.

Finding that they were dealing with a full-blown cell of ten jihadists made some members of the task force rejoice, but it had the opposite effect on Becky. Of course, it was a great thing to take out ten terrorists—assuming her guys in Raleigh found the driver of the van. What if he'd moved on to another city and they were wasting precious time? What if all of it had been a ploy to pull Sanchez away because they somehow knew they were being watched and wanted to divert the EOD tech away from the larger number of explosives? Something else was still afoot. Some of them had been whispering that it didn't matter if they couldn't take out the hospitals and communications, because all they really had to do was prove they could place "the real weapon."

When one of the men sneered at the deputy processing him and mumbled that he'd soon know the sting of death, Becky didn't know if she should assume the man spoke in a general sense or that he meant "the real weapon" would kill the officer standing right in front of him. She didn't have to mull over it for more than five seconds, because the terrorist began to describe in detail all that would happen to the deputy before he took his last breath. The final words of his threat roughly translated, "It will reach you in less than two days."

Becky made for the door, literally slamming into Conor Flynn in her haste.

"Outside," she hissed, breathing against the panic that began to build in her chest. Matt stood talking to Kael and Declan, cheeks turning red when he noticed her speed-walking toward them.

"We were just talking about you, Chief." Declan slapped Matt on the shoulder.

"There's a bioweapon." Becky ignored Declan entirely.

All of the men tensed. Footsteps crunched on the ground, approaching quickly.

Rob called out to them, "They located the van. It's heading toward the capital building in Raleigh. Local PD has blocked and cleared all possible routes, and they have a sniper ready to take out the driver on approach."

"I need Sanchez on comms," Becky croaked, feeling nauseous. "NOW!"

A tornado of activity blew all around Matt, and he hadn't felt so helpless and on edge since the time he'd been pinned down for what his platoon sergeant later referred to as "the hour from hell." He alternated between pacing the floor of Town Hall and sitting with his knees bouncing and his hands aching to shoot something.

When word came that the van was making its approach toward the capital, the room grew quiet. No one seemed to breathe as the scene played out in broken communications and endless moments waiting for the next string of words.

Finally, confirmation was sent that the driver had taken a sniper's bullet to the head. The van didn't blow. Sanchez and the backup he'd acquired moved on the van, opened it, and confirmed there was an explosive ordnance. Still, it didn't blow.

"All clear." The words should have brought him peace, but that earlier feeling—that it had all been too easy—plagued him again.

"No. Something isn't right." Becky said the words that kept running on a loop in Matt's head. They were still missing a piece of the puzzle.

"Why do you always have to make things more dramatic than they are?" Rob groaned. "You heard it yourself from the guy you handpicked. It was a regular device with no purpose beyond going boom."

"This. Is. Not. Over." Becky ground out each word. "We have to comb through every spec of evidence we recovered from that house."

"My guys are already on it." Rob gestured to five agents huddled in the back of the room. He and Becky continued to argue, but Matt tuned them out. Walking to where the agents were flipping through stacks of paper, Matt tried and failed to read a single word of the script. He recognized it from his years in the Middle East, but he never had been able to make heads or tails of it.

A minute later, Becky brushed by him, plopping down to do what he presumed would be most of the actual legwork. One of the five FBI agents paused as he looked through documents. He was clearly reading the page in his hand, but he had yet to indicate whether he understood the implications of what was written on it.

"Does this make any sense to you, Salazar?" The man spoke, holding up a map of the Pisgah National Forest.

"It's a map of where they were staying." Becky squinted at it. "What's that written on it?"

"Here where the house is, it says 'base.' But what's this, up near the parkway?"

Becky took the map and looked closely. "Does that say 'the trial'?"

"I think you're right." The man took back the map, looking again. "I was going to say 'the test,' but you're the expert."

Just then, three fresh faces entered the room, and Becky jumped to her feet. She walked straight into the tight embrace of a woman with hair as red as the three Flynn brothers. Clearly this new influx of people were some that Becky worked with on a regular basis. They wasted no time, displacing the FBI agents and scouring over the evidence with ease. In no time, they had set up a system that Matt couldn't begin to understand, and after watching them for a full ten minutes, he snapped out of his trance, rubbing his blurry eyes and fighting the urge to put his fist through a wall. He had to find some way to be useful or he'd very well lose his mind.

Becky caught his eye when she looked wearily up at him for a moment, then she slumped back over, staring at a notebook in her hand.

A smile pulled at his mouth when he thought of the one thing he had to offer in the moment. He turned toward the door, nodding for Conor to follow him out of it.

"What's up?" Conor sounded as exhausted as the rest of the team who'd either stayed awake the entire night or barely slept with the anticipation of the early morning op.

"We're going to see my friend Oscar. I think everyone could use breakfast burritos and coffee, don't you?" Matt shoved the door open and fished in his pocket for the keys to his cruiser.

"I was thinking donuts, but now that the mountain air is hitting my face and I'm realizing I'm not likely to make it back to Declan's house for my mom's famous pancake sausages on a stick, a burrito might just hit the spot."

"Pancake sausages on a stick? That sounds disgusting."

Conor laughed. "It does, but if you ever have one, you'll change your tune."

"Rob would tell you everything is fine and you should go have your stick of breakfast delight." Matt smirked over the hood of the cruiser, unlocking the doors so they could slide into the cold seats.

"Rob is about as useful as a trapdoor in a canoe." Conor sat down in the passenger seat.

"Ha! I'm definitely stealing that to use on my cousin." Matt cranked the cruiser, tapping the seat warmer buttons and turning the vents on full blast. "She'll love it. Which reminds me, I need to let her know it's safe for Penny to head home."

"Why don't you hold off on that?" Conor shook his head. "I'm not entirely convinced that it is."

"No?" Matt's heart rate kicked up. "No, I don't suppose it is until we know what has Becky believing this isn't over."

"Butter my butt and call me a biscuit." Petty Officer Second Class Kennedy O'Brien punched Becky's shoulder. "Who is that, and can I take him home when I leave?"

Becky turned to see Matt and Conor walking into HQ with arms full of sustenance. Conor had a box of what looked like burritos wrapped individually in foil. Matt, of course, had coffee. He balanced two produce boxes that had been repurposed into drink carriers for copious amounts of the caffeinated nectar. An FBI agent near the doorway jumped into action, relieving Matt of one box. When he placed the other on the table at the front of the room, he removed a cup and looked up, eyes landing on Becky a moment before his feet started carrying him straight toward her.

"Ooohhh." O'Brien chuckled under her breath. "I can see he's already taken. Is that your deputy?"

"Sure enough. And don't you forget it." Becky chewed on her bottom lip as Matt held the coffee out to her. After she'd taken the cup and let the first gulp of perfectly delectable liquid coat her insides with energizing warmth, she rasped out, "You really light up my life, Sunshine. I think I'll keep you."

O'Brien snorted and kicked her under the table. "Who the heck are you, and what have you done with my grouch of a friend?"

"Matt, this is Petty Officer O'Brien." Becky nodded her head toward the ginger.

"Matt Taylor." He spoke his name, holding out his hand toward O'Brien. She smiled too sweetly when she shook it.

"Friends call me Ken, but you can call me anything you want, handso—"

Becky kicked her friend back, harder than she should have, and glared with a look that said, "MINE."

O'Brien cleared her throat loudly and corrected herself. "Call me O'Brien."

"Nice to meet you, O'Brien." Matt pursed his lips, clearly amused.

Becky took another sip of her coffee, cheeks warming from the heat of the beverage and her mini tantrum.

"Guess I'll get my own cup of joe." O'Brien stood with a knowing look on her face. "I've heard all about your coffee brewing skills, Matt. Did you make this batch yourself?"

"Afraid not."

"Hmmm." O'Brien pouted. "That's too bad."

"Hurry along and get your go-juice, O'Brien." Becky raised an eyebrow. "You're clearly not focused on the task at hand."

O'Brien narrowed her eyes, saying, "Roger, Chief."

"She seems extra nice." Matt sat in the chair O'Brien had vacated.

"Nice is one way to put it. A shameless flirt is way more accurate." Becky shrugged, realizing in that moment that she had a type. "Actually, she's the female version of you."

"Ah, I see. I thought she looked like a kindred spirit." He rested his forearms on the table. "She's the best friend ever, isn't she? Someone you simply can't live without."

"Something like that."

Becky wished she had time to actually flirt with the guy who, when this was all over—not Rob's version of "close enough" to over—she had every intention of pursuing just as hard as he'd been pursuing her for . . . had it really only been three days? Tomorrow was Christmas Eve. Either they really had thwarted the terrorists and the next two days would be as merry as any other year, or they'd missed something and the Grinch's diabolical plans for Whoville would pale in comparison to what they'd figure out too late. The confidence of the terrorists sitting in county lockup didn't bode well at all.

O'Brien's familiar energy infiltrated the bubble that Becky wished could remain around her and Matt.

"Look, I know I'm prone to exaggeration. But this is the single best cup of coffee I've ever tasted." O'Brien shot an accusatory look at Matt. "You're sure you didn't make it?"

"Positive." Matt chuckled.

O'Brien settled into the chair on Becky's other side, probably forgetting all about the emails she was supposed to be reading on the laptop the feds found in Penny's guesthouse. The receipts and correspondences should be easy enough to sort through, seeing as most of them were in English. The travel confirmations for some of the men they had in custody at the jail were one more detail that was throwing Becky off her axis. They must have been planning to scatter and possibly regroup at a later date to carry out another attack. The five men without itineraries must've never intended to survive the IEDs.

The most alarming discovery was the name of the man they hadn't previously identified and who they absolutely did not have in custody. A Pakistani national whose picture didn't match any of the faces she'd studied this morning. She already had Homeland Security assets deployed to apprehend him later today, assuming he showed up to the airport for his flight. Why was it set for earlier than the rest of his men?

Putting her alarm aside, she refocused on O'Brien's declaration about the coffee.

"It's the water." Becky smiled at Matt, feeling like she'd taken partial ownership of Appalachia with the statement that came naturally to locals. The words got stuck in her brain for a moment.

It's the water.

"The water," she gasped, jumping from her seat and shoving her cup into Matt's hand. She rushed around the table to where the stack of maps had been abandoned. "Matt!"

He was at her side in an instant.

"Call Whit. We need her." Becky stood fully upright, praying she was wrong and knowing without a doubt that she was absolutely right. "It's the water. That's why they were on the trail. That's why they have so many maps of forests and grasslands all over the country. I thought it was their idea of places to lay low, but it's got to be the key to everything."

Matt had his phone to his ear, saying, "Hey, Granny. Can you put Whit on the line?"

Becky stared at Courthouse Falls on the map, taking a step to her left when O'Brien peered over her shoulder.

"The trial," O'Brien read aloud. "That's . . . foreboding."

Becky whipped around to grab Matt's shoulder. "Tell her we'll come there as soon as we can, actually. We've got to get eyes on Courthouse Falls first."

"Did you hear that?" Matt spoke into the phone. After a couple of seconds, he said, "Stay put. It won't do us any good for you to be in the mix until we know what we're dealing with. I mean it, Whit. We'll come to you."

Chapter 13

12:50 P.M. - PISGAH NATIONAL FOREST

THE FINAL MILE OF the drive to the trailhead felt like an eternity. When they got close enough to see a Subaru parked on the side of the road, Matt almost swore an oath. The familiar logos littering the back of the vehicle sent a mix of confusion and dread into his racing thoughts. What were the odds that the "I love hugging trees" and "828 is great" stickers were just a cover for whoever was driving that vehicle?

"Do you see what I see?" Becky gaped at the Subaru.

"We assumed the car was Alice and Zach's ride," Matt said. "Maybe it wasn't . . ." He stopped mid-theory, catching sight of the driver still sitting in the car. He looked like a Zach, with pale skin and light brown hair sticking out of a multicolor trapper hat. Regardless, he wasn't Middle Eastern. The guy, maybe nineteen or twenty years old, drummed on his steering wheel and nodded his head to whatever music was playing inside the vehicle. He coughed, a telltale puff of thick smoke coming from his mouth when he saw Matt's cruiser stopped right next to him. It definitely wasn't a regular cigarette in his hand.

By the time Matt jumped out and rushed toward the car, the kid had his window down and his hands held up in front of him. The stench of marijuana wafting out of his car made Matt gag, but he ignored it and leaned over.

"I-I was, um—"

"Are you Zach?" Matt's question made the guy's mouth as round as his eyes.

"Whoa, how'd you know that?"

"Have you seen this man here today?" Matt held up his phone, a picture of Yazan Masood—the missing Pakistani terrorist—on the screen. A Toyota 4-Runner pulled over behind Zach's Subaru, and Matt was about to yell at Whit to get back home when Zach confirmed the worst possible news.

"YaYa!" Zach said affectionately. "I mean, yes, sir. I saw Yazan walking on the side of the road and picked him up. He's gone to the falls to take some pictures. I guess the lighting was bad last time he was here. I'm giving him a ride to the airport when he's done."

"Oh yeah? Driving him to the airport . . . after sitting here getting high?" Matt raised his eyebrows.

"Uhhhh," Zach's panicked thoughts were on full display.

"When did he start down the trail?" Becky demanded.

"Man." Zach glanced at the clock on his infotainment screen, then smiled. "Seven minutes ago. Yeah. I remember because he pointed at the time and told me he'd be back in exactly two hours. I told him there was no rush."

"How long have you known Masood?" Matt narrowed his eyes.

"Who?" Zach stared at him in confusion.

To clarify, Matt bit out, "Yazan."

"Oh." Zach nodded. "Officially, less than half an hour. But I sort of met him on the trail the other day."

"And why are you so keen to help him out? Sounds like you're old friends." Matt actually believed the idiot, but surely not even Zach was that braindead.

"Hey, man, I'm trying to be neighborly. A friend of mine was rude to him." He shrugged. "It's up to me to show him Americans aren't all the same, ya know?"

Matt met Becky's eyes.

"We have to find him." She stated the obvious and kept on stating it. "You need to call for a ride, Zach, if you can get any service up here. In fact, call Alice and tell her she was right. You're an idiot and she was right to trust her instincts. You need to get out of here, but don't drive."

"Becky, call in our location and have Conor send backup." Matt had half a mind to contradict her and tell Zach to stay exactly where he was until someone could escort him to the county jail, but he had bigger problems than a pothead on the parkway. "Masood is a terrorist, Zach. You may have helped him kill people today. You need to report to the sheriff's department and tell them everything you did. If you don't, best believe I'll be knocking on your door, messing up your Christmas."

Whit was to them before Zach could form a reply. At least the kid looked thoroughly shaken up and seemed to buy into Matt's bluff about coming to his home. He was nodding his head and looked like he might throw up.

"What's going on?" Whit's hands landed on her hips. "You said you needed me."

"I told you to stay home, actually," Matt growled.

"I'm here now," Whit persisted.

"We need to walk and talk. As much as I want to wring your neck, we really do need your expertise."

"Backup is on the way." Becky was already moving toward the trailhead.

They booked it down the trail without as much as a backward glance at Zach when he called out a farewell.

"Whit, what would happen if someone put a contaminant in the water at the falls?" Matt asked, lungs already burning with the cold air moving in and out.

"Depends on what you're talking about. Like a toxin?"

"A bioweapon," Becky blurted out.

"Again, depends on what it is and—" Whit was going to overanalyze every detail if Matt didn't keep her on track.

"Let's assume we're dealing with something perfectly weaponized and expertly designed, Whit." He jumped over a puddle of frozen mud. "If it makes it downstream, how many people are getting sick?"

"This is the headwater for the French Broad. That travels throughout the state, then into Tennessee. Then dumps into the Ohio River and the Mississippi from there."

"God, please let us get to him in time." Becky breathed a prayer. "Say it makes it into the Mississippi. How many people do you think that affects, roughly?"

"Drinking water . . . north of twenty million." Whit started to slow her speech, seeming to finally grasp the severity of what might happen. "But it's not only the drinking water at that point. If it's a strong enough weapon, a bacteria that can travel that far in freezing waters—we're looking at agricultural and industrial ramifications too."

"The hospitals and communications." Becky sounded breathless as she spoke. "Do you think they were trying to stop people from being treated so they'd die, Matt?"

"What's this about hospitals and communications?" Whit cut in.

"They had plans to place bombs all over the county and beyond." Matt filled in the blank.

"Hmm." Whit hummed. "Taking out hospitals would definitely mean a higher death toll. But with it being a bioweapon and taking out cell towers and the internet, it sounds to me like they were trying to delay the weaponized bacteria from being identified in a timely manner."

"That . . . is the most logical thing I think you've ever said, Whit."

"Everything I say is logical," she retorted. "You just don't know how to listen to reason. You know where you get that from, right?"

Her underlying message hit him in the gut. She wasn't talking about a terrorist attack anymore.

"How is my mother?"

"She's not great, Matty." The use of Penny's old nickname for him was intentional. "She needs her son to be as stubborn and persistent at pursuing her as he is with everything else he wants."

"Stay. Put," Matt hissed to his cousin before turning toward Becky, his eyes flashing in the sunshine that streamed through the trees.

"Don't think for one second I'm staying behind," Becky whispered, listening for another indication that Masood was nearby, like the stomping footsteps that had made them all pause. "I have to see this through."

Matt eyed the Glock 19 in her grip and surprised her when he nodded without protest and turned to lead in the last stretch of the trail. They'd stopped talking midway through the hike when they had asked Whit all the ecological questions they could think of on the spot.

A man's cough on the trail ahead was the only indication they were about to stumble on a terrorist willing to wipe out millions of Americans. When they rounded a grouping of trees and caught sight of the back of Masood, he glanced over his shoulder and broke into a run toward the creek bed that led up to the waterfall. Matt and Becky stayed hot on his heels.

Slow is smooth, smooth is fast . . .

Her stupid inner voice picked the worst possible moment to mimic the Navy SEALs she'd worked with over the years. But those guys weren't wrong.

"Masood! Don't do it." Matt came to a screeching halt several yards from the icy water, weapon raised.

Catching up to him, Becky held her breath and prayed with all her might. Masood stood beside the water's edge, holding a metallic canister in his hand. He had gone to more effort to blend in than the other terrorists they'd extracted from Penny's property, being way more clean-cut and put together. It was no wonder Zach fell for the man's ruse—he wore a red ball cap and a flannel shirt similar to the one Matt had worn the first time they were on this trail, and he actually had a leather camera bag on this shoulder, but his eyes were just as hate-filled as in the one picture they had of him.

The angry defeat on Masood's face gave Becky hope that he would put the canister down without a fight. The seconds they stood staring at each other seemed to tick by in slow motion, only the birds chirping and rushing sound of the water were indications that time hadn't stopped completely.

Finally, a flash of determination crossed his face. He jerked the lid off the canister and yelled, "*Allahu*—"

Matt's shot rang out before Masood could finish the declaration.

He fell to the ground in a crumpled heap, crimson seeping from his chest, staining what little snow was on the ground. Becky didn't hesitate, barely hearing Matt yell for her to stop. She rushed to the canister, replacing the lid before she could process that doing so might mean certain death.

Matt pulled her backward, putting himself between her and the canister and Masood. He said nothing as he kicked Masood's body into the supine position and checked for a pulse. When it was obvious that Masood wasn't breathing—ever again—Matt turned to Becky with fury in his eyes.

"What did you do?"

"I-I couldn't risk it getting to the water." She pointed at the canister.

"You shouldn't have touched it. Backup is—"

"Not here yet, Matt." She cut him off. "Every second counts. We don't know what it is."

"Exactly," he said through gritted teeth and looked at her hands. "I'd tell you to wash your hands off, but . . ."

Becky snorted.

"Don't do that." He shook his head, as serious as she'd seen him. "It isn't funny, Rebecca."

"Oohhh." She couldn't help herself. Maybe she'd die from whatever was on her hands. But the endorphins coursing through her body after forty-five minutes of exertion and the sheer relief of having stopped Masood before he released his weapon overcame her. "You sounded like Rob just then."

"You. Are. Not. Funny." He punctuated each word.

"Man, I'd really love to kiss you right about now."

"Because you want me to shut up or because you want to take me with you when you go?" The severity of his glare was starting to fade.

"I think I want to spend the rest of my life with you, Matthew Taylor. However long it is." She took a deep breath and glanced at the waterfall she hadn't yet admired. It glistened more than Matt's green eyes, the white water falling over impossibly smooth rock. The smell of damp earth filled her lungs and calmed her spirit. It was beautiful. "Right here in these mountains. Heck, maybe at the base of this waterfall."

"That's dark." Matt was shaking his head when she looked back at him. "There's something seriously wrong with you."

She hummed a laugh, knowing she wasn't the only one. "I think you like it."

His lips twitched as a stampede of boots stomped and Whit's voice rang above the voices of a swarm of FBI agents, Homeland Security, and all other manner of operatives.

"Oh, good," Whit called out over the chaos marring what had been a perfectly serene place moments prior. "You'uns didn't die."

"Yet," Matt said before his lips pursed and he fought a smile. Then he shook his head. "No. It's not funny."

"It's a little funny." Becky shrugged, wishing she didn't need to keep her hands to herself.

Becky nudged a twig and some leaves with the toe of her boot, heaving a sigh. The soothing sound of the nearby waterfall had stopped being helpful after the first ten minutes of endless waiting. At least she knew the headquarters down in Rosman was finally in an appropriate state of productivity and hustle—according to the muffled message Conor had relayed through the wall of the negative pressure tent. Becky had been shoved into it with nothing more than her disinfected phone, which was useless for anything other than telling her how many hours had passed. She sighed, glancing at the phone's clock for the umpteenth time since she'd been quarantined for tests to be run on whatever she'd hastily touched in her effort to save millions of lives.

The discovery of antibiotics in Masood's "camera bag" hopefully meant that whatever they'd both handled was actually treatable. He'd had an airline ticket booked to go to Montana this very afternoon, which she surmised he'd intended to visit for the same purpose he'd come to North Carolina. Every place they'd flagged as a target on the terrorists' list had headwaters just like Courthouse Falls. If Masood had been on a suicide mission, handling a contagion that didn't have a cure, he likely would have flown into a place like D.C., New York, or Los Angeles.

The door on the temporary Army structure unzipped, and a woman entered without personal protective gear. Her bright white coat and neon pink stethoscope matched the confident energy she put off. The CAC card she wore in a lanyard around her neck and the boots she had on her feet reminded Becky of the severity of her situation.

"Colonel Roper, at your service," the colonel quipped with a smile, causing Becky to suck in a breath, eyes immediately burning with a rush of relieved tears.

She knew what the tall blonde officer would say before the words left her lips, but hearing them spoken aloud was the Christmas miracle Becky had been silently praying for during the last three hours.

"You're going to be fine, Chief Salazar. No traces of Francisella tularemis were detected on your clothes or skin or on the outside of the canister it was being stored in. And even if you had been exposed, it's treatable."

"Francisella?" Becky interrupted when the doctor took a breath. "What would that have caused exactly?"

"Tularemia—also known as rabbit fever. You might have presented with flu-like symptoms, skin ulcers, swollen lymph nodes . . . stuff like that. But thankfully it seems as though the weaponized bacillus would have had to make it into the water for the protective layer around it to dissolve and flow downstream. It would have been a very unmerry Christmas for a lot of folks."

"Oh, thank God we got here in time." Becky hugged herself. "I don't get it. Why didn't they use something stronger?"

"I wouldn't call it a weak weapon. It's a doozy of a plan you thwarted." Colonel Roper rocked back on her heels. "They really thought of everything. We would have been looking at a bacteria that is resistant to freezing and chlorine, that multiplies in mud and water, and that could possibly survive for months. It spreads like wildfire in animals and humans, and if we hadn't figured out what we were dealing with in a timely manner, we'd have had an epidemic on our hands with a lot of lives lost."

Becky digested the information, shivering with the thought of how close they'd come to disaster. They weren't entirely in the clear, needing to take all they'd learned and broaden their mission objectives to encompass a nationwide hunt for any other cells that may be gearing up to contaminate other headwaters. They already knew Montana, Colorado, and North and South Dakota were on the list. How many more headwaters were there to worry about? Thankfully, they had access to unlimited resources now that the threat was understood to be so much broader than one tiny town in western North Carolina. They'd also gained the full attention of every powerhead in the country all the way up to the Commander in Chief.

"Thank you, ma'am. Am I free to go?" Becky stood, hesitating to hold out her hand, having considered herself a carrier of some sort of plague for three too many hours. The colonel stepped closer, offering her hand first and shaking Becky's firmly.

"You are, and I'm sorry to tell you that there's no rest for the weary. I overheard a hothead on the radio saying he needed to get you back down the mountain. Sounded like a fed on a power trip." She rolled her eyes. "Those guys are the worst. All bark—and no bite when it counts."

"Yes ma'am." Becky laughed, knowing without a doubt it was Rob whom the colonel had heard.

She thanked the woman again and moved toward the door, exhaustion washing over her now that she knew she wasn't as likely to take the long nap anytime soon. Maybe she could close her eyes for the drive, though part of her feared it would be the last chance she would have to take in the beautiful Blue Ridge scenery for who knew how long, and that caused a pit to open up in her stomach.

Chapter 14

4:40 P.M. COURTHOUSE FALLS

MATT PACED THE FOREST floor, staring at the tent the Army colonel had gone into several minutes prior. She wasn't wearing a mask or gloves and hadn't bothered to zip the door after entering. That had to be a good sign. The moment Becky stepped out ahead of the colonel, looking weary but relieved, his feet carried him toward her more swiftly than when he'd been pursuing Masood.

Becky caught sight of him and took two steps in his direction before he engulfed her in a tight embrace. Breathing in the faint scent of vanilla from her hair, he couldn't gather his racing thoughts enough to string two words together.

Becky tilted her head back and grinned up at him.

"You waited for me."

"Obviously." He finally remembered how to speak.

"Do you want the good news or bad news first?"

"Why does there have to be bad news?" He scowled. "No. I refuse to hear it."

"Okay, the good news then." She pursed her lips for a beat. "I'm not gonna die. At least not from any freaky terrorist bacteria."

"I gathered as much from the sudden release and the smile." His heart began to calm as reality caught up with him. "I'm not just a pretty face with a gun and killer personality, Chief. I also happen to possess a smidgeon of deductive reasoning."

"Smidgeon is a conservative estimate. I already established that you're smarter than you look, or don't you remember?"

He fought to temper his growing smile and gave her a sufficient glare. "Every time it sounds like you're giving me a compliment, there's a follow-up smack to my ego."

"I think your ego will be fine." She smiled at him for a moment before she delivered the bad news he'd insisted he didn't want to hear. "I have to get back to HQ. The work isn't over and . . . I have a feeling I'm going to be swept up and out of your hair—which isn't as bad as I initially thought, by the way—in a day or two. The next twenty-four hours are going to be crucial. We have to deploy teams to every possible target area."

"What's wrong with my hair?" He scoffed, trying not to show how hard the other words hit him.

"You know good and well that mop wouldn't pass any regulations anywhere, Taylor." She shook her head in disapproval before her lips twitched. "Though it has its uses."

"Like what?"

"Like . . ." Her arms wrapped around his neck, tugging him closer, and her fingers slid into his hair as she whispered on his lips, "It gives me something to hold on to, for starters."

Their lips met in the kiss he'd been planning in the back of his mind since the minute their first had ended in uncomfortable chiding from Conor Flynn. This kiss wasn't filled with the same intensity as the one in his truck, when they'd been high on emotions and the threat of the unknown. Instead there was a calm steadiness to the way Becky kissed him, like it wouldn't be the last time. The rightness of their connection filled him with an inexplicable peace, despite knowing he couldn't hold onto her for long. She was leaving, but *maybe* she'd be back. Or maybe God meant for Matt to follow her. One thing he knew for sure, he wasn't letting her slip away this time.

When a throat cleared near them, bringing their liplock to an end, neither of them looked to see who was trying to get their attention. Matt rested his forehead on hers and took a deep breath.

"We belong together. You know that, right?"

She slowly let her fingers slide to his chest, head nodding in agreement. "Granny said so, after all."

"Will you give me Christmas Day?"

"I'll ask Uncle Sam." She grinned up at him when he stood to his full height again. "He owes me one, so I'm optimistic."

Turning toward the person who was waiting for them, Matt's eyebrows shot up when he took in Special Agent Robert Simms' resigned expression.

"You're both needed at HQ, if you're ready to head back." Rob shoved his hands into his pockets, and Matt braced himself for whatever Becky would say.

"Thanks, Robert." Her tone didn't hold any malice or even an edge of annoyance. "We will head back in a minute."

Rob gave a singular nod and walked away, directing his steps toward the colonel who had cleared Becky to leave.

"That was the most civility I've seen between you two." Matt met Becky's gaze.

"I'm over it." She shrugged dismissively and stepped right back into his arms. "What's the point in holding a grudge when I've found something so much better to hold on to?"

He laughed and looked to the sky. "I don't ever want to hear how I'm the sappy romcom fanatic again. Do you even hear yourself, Chief?"

Becky slapped his arm but joined in his laughter for a moment. "Turns out, you're the one who was carrying something contagious."

His laughter faded when he stared into rich brown eyes and really let her words sink in. "I'm not letting you off the hook for all you said earlier."

"You mean the spending my life with you in Appalachia thing?"

He nodded.

She hummed, her cheeks darkening with a blush. "I meant what I said. Perspective is a beautiful thing, isn't it?"

"Are you talking about how life is short? Or how I'm such a huge improvement from the last guy?"

"Both." She aimed an incredulous stare up at him. "Obviously."

"Speaking of . . ." Matt whispered. "Should we warn the colonel about Rob?"

A snort escaped Becky, and she shook her head. "Nah. She can handle him just fine. We've got way bigger fish to fry down the mountain. Get ready for another long night and day, Marine."

"You really ought to get some rest, Chief."

"We can sleep when we're dead." She pursed her lips when he narrowed his eyes.

"You have the darkest humor of anyone I know, and that's saying a lot with my list of acquaintances."

"What do you expect from someone who spends all her time around guys like you?" She shrugged unapologetically. "You boys made me this way."

"I'm not the only one full of surprises, am I?" He took a step back and grabbed her hand when she held it out to him.

"You have no idea." Her cheeks rounded in a mischievous smile when she tugged him toward the trail. "Let's get out of here before the sun goes down and the ghost of Bambi comes to stalk us."

CHRISTMAS MORNING

Becky sat up in bed, mind disoriented and pulse racing. She was late for something. How had she slept through her alarm? What day was it? And why did she smell coffee? Movement in the kitchen of her rented cabin sent a rush of panic through her. She'd locked the doors up tight before collapsing into a deep sleep.

A murderer probably wouldn't bother brewing coffee before offing her. What else was wafting through the walls? A sweet cinnamon fragrance made her mouth water and motivated her enough to stumble to the bathroom to brush her teeth.

When she stepped out of the bedroom, wrapping a decorative throw blanket around herself, she stopped in her tracks, seeing the fireplace in use for the first time. A fully decorated Christmas tree sat in the corner, and she wondered how in the world she'd slept through the noise of someone—someone with boundary issues—turning her cabin into the perfect scene for a Hallmark movie. Then she remembered the exhaustion of two sleepless nights. It was a wonder she was on her feet even now.

Warm arms wrapped around her from behind and a light kiss landed above her ear before Matt whispered, "Merry Christmas, Chief. Don't shoot."

She turned in his arms and rested her cheek on his chest. After a minute of soaking in his warmth, she narrowed her eyes and looked up at him.

"How did you get in here?"

"I have my ways." He shrugged.

"You know, for a respected member of the law enforcement community, you don't seem overly committed to following the letter of the law."

"Man's laws don't supersede matters of the heart."

"Yes. They absolutely do." She shook her head, not believing her ears. "Imagine the chaos that would ensue if everyone took that devil-may-care attitu—"

Matt lips landed on hers, cutting off her half-hearted tantrum. Then he said, "My cousin sent me the code to the door. He—"

"Don't say it." She laughed. "I don't have the brain space to contemplate how you're related to everyone in Appalachia. You all run some sort of hillbilly mafia, monopolizing every industry."

Matt studied her face as if trying to understand what he was looking at. "It's got to be exhausting, living in a steady state of suspicion and conspiracy theories."

"I'm sure it's not half as enjoyable as being a hopeless romantic, but it pays the bills and saves the day from time to time . . . so there's that."

"Speaking of being romantic and saving the day, I made breakfast." Matt walked backward, pulling her with him when he grabbed the blanket she was wrapped in. "My specialty—made from scratch cinnamon rolls."

Becky bent forward, laughing loudly, and by the looks of it, surprising Matt with her sudden outburst.

"Why are you laughing maniacally?" He sounded on the verge of agitation.

"Cinnamon rolls. Oh, you really are funny."

Surely he saw the parallel of the most commonly cast male character type. Like the breakfast food that easily doubled as a dessert, the warm, sweet, gooey center was the perfect depiction of her fast hero.

"I'm not following." His blond eyebrows pulled together.

Becky sighed contentedly and snuggled back into his arms.

"You're perfect, Matthew Taylor. Exactly what I never knew I always needed."

"God knew. And Granny." Matt nodded his head.

"Exactly," she agreed. "I'm not letting you go this time. I don't know what it'll look like, but if you keep plying me with delicious coffee and home-cooked meals, I'll move heaven and earth to make this happen."

"Is that all it took to get you to come to your senses? I could have made cinnamon rolls the very first morning."

Becky grabbed a fistful of his flannel shirt and shut him up the best way she knew how.

Epilogue

ONE YEAR LATER

MATT WATCHED AS HIS wife sipped on a candy cane milkshake and absentmindedly rubbed her five-month pregnant belly, window shopping through the streets of Brevard, North Carolina. The Christmas music in the distance, the twinkling of lights overhead, and the excited chatter of families enjoying the final hours of the street festival put a smile on his face. None of the people surrounding them had the first clue that three hundred and sixty-four days ago, his then-girlfriend selflessly threw her life on the line in a desperate attempt to keep them blissfully ignorant to the darkness that lurked just beyond their happy homes.

The terror had gotten way too close, coming full circle and nearly decimating the American population on an even larger scale than when the whole world watched the attacks that made this sovereign nation turn to a decades-long war in the first place. They should have been better prepared for a significant shift in tactics prior to that, which is exactly what Becky had said in front of a slew of congressmen.

It was arrogant and dangerous to live under the assumption that we could restrict these sorts of attacks to foreign soil. The American people deserve better from all of us.

He teared up every time he thought about her closing statement.

"You're doing it again." Becky didn't look at him as she took another long drag of the sugary, milky goodness that they were supposed to be sharing.

"Doing what?" He feigned ignorance, knowing she could see right through him.

He couldn't help it. He'd been all up in his feelings since she came home from her final out-of-town assignment last week. From here on out, she'd be analyzing and consulting for the Department of Defense from the safety of their Appalachian home. No longer a chief in the United States Navy, Rebecca Taylor had traded in her insignia and boots for mountain water coffee and motherhood.

"You know exactly what, Matthew Taylor." She finally turned her brown eyes on him. "Stop thinking about last year and . . . go get another milkshake. I've pretty much finished this one, and I know how much you love chomping on the bits of candy cane like a horse with a sugar cube."

Alarm flooded his chest as silver rims of tears appeared in her eyes. "Hey . . . what's wrong?"

"Nothing." She stomped her foot. "I'm just so happy."

"Oh, yeah. You're the picture of joy." He framed her face with his hands and swiped his thumb on her cheek, catching the single tear that fell. "Is it hormones or something else?"

"You're asking me? I'm not the emotional one." She sucked in a shuddered breath. "You're the expert here."

"I love when you compliment me by shattering my ego, baby." He pursed his lips.

"I love when you call me baby." Her tears evaporated as quickly as they'd appeared, and she batted her eyelashes at him as she took another sip of the milkshake.

"Stop!" a lady yelled from the doorway of the old-fashioned soda shoppe, throwing her hands in the air when a ragged-looking older man ran right by Matt and Becky on the sidewalk. "Get back here!"

"Everything okay, CeeCee?" Becky asked the owner of the establishment.

"That guy pulled a dine and dash. Dirty miscreant," CeeCee growled, deflating and slipping back into the restaurant.

Becky smacked Matt on the chest. "Aren't you going to run after him, Deputy?"

"I'm off duty." Matt watched as the man struggled to jog, rounding the corner at the toy store. "Besides, he's headed straight toward the police department. I'll let them handle—"

Becky scoffed and shoved his arm. "Matthew Taylor, so help me! A criminal just absconded with a belly full of stolen goods."

"I'm going, I'm going." Matt laughed. "I'm giving him a head start. You saw the guy. He needs this."

"You're not funny." Becky shook her head, turning purposefully in the direction the man had gone. "I'll do it myself."

"The heck you will." He jogged around her, yelling over his shoulder, "Get me another milkshake and tell CeeCee I'll handle it."

Making her way back into the soda shoppe, Becky sat down and heaved a sigh. Who knew growing a human would be more physically exhausting than wearing full gear for an op in the dead of summer? She needed a bubble bath, a foot massage, and maybe she'd be the one to demand a snuggle on the couch. Slowing down and being intentional about affection didn't come as naturally to her as it did to Matt, but either she was changing or the attempted coup by her hormones was working.

Of all the places she'd been in her life, nothing rivaled the quaint, festive, close-knit community of Appalachia. The Christmas music and laughter inside the soda shoppe filled her heart to bursting.

A waitress took her simple order and disappeared, leaving Becky to soak up the merry vibes of the season. A young couple nearby seemed to be on a date. They reminded her of a younger version of herself and Matt, right down to the Marine Corps logo tattooed on the guy's forearm. He couldn't have been a Marine for long, looking no older than twenty. What would it have been like to date Matt when they were that young and just starting out in their military careers? The guy pulled a long black velvet box from inside his coat and whatever piece of jewelry rested inside had the girl moving into his side of the booth, crying and acting as if there was mistletoe above them.

"Becky?" A woman quietly called her name, then tapped her on the shoulder. Looking up, Becky's heart nearly stopped, seeing her mother-in-law not only far from the security of Balsam Grove, but smiling brightly at her. Penny looked so different—put together and not the least bit skittish or angry at bumping into someone who reminded her of pain and loss.

"Penny." Becky moved to stand.

"Don't get up." Penny waved her hands. "Could I . . . sit for a minute?"

"Of course." Becky nodded, gesturing to the other side of the booth. "Matt will be back soon."

Penny nodded, glancing toward the entrance. "I liked the invitation to your wedding. It was pretty. Nice that you all had it at Courthouse Falls. I love it up there, especially in early summer."

Becky gulped, then blurted out, "We wish you could have been there."

Penny met her gaze and took a deep breath. "I was there."

"Oh." Becky blinked in confusion. How could they have missed her? Only a few dozen people had made the trek with them.

"I went early and kept out of sight," Penny supplied. "Didn't want to cause a scene."

"How—how are you, Penny?"

"Healing. Whit found someone to help me after how I acted at Christmas, and I've been working hard to navigate through . . . everything." Her face fell, and she studied her hands folded on the table in front of her. "I let so many years slip by. I lost my son, and according to Whit, if I don't fix what's broken, I may never get to know my granddaughter. I know it's Matty who's been cleaning up around the house, but every time I hear him park his truck, I'm too terrified to face him. The way I hurt him all those years, it's unforgivable."

"Penny—" Becky's voice cracked. The blasted hormones were going to get the best of her. "You didn't lose Matt. All he wants is to have his mom back, but I think he's afraid too. He doesn't want to make it worse by forcing anything and hurting *you* more."

"He won't. It's not his fault, but I know I made him believe it was." She took a deep breath. "They put me on some medicine. I can't say I don't ever have bad days, but I do feel like myself again. Does that make sense?"

"Of course."

"And I'm going to church with Whit and Jeannie. That helps a lot." Penny blinked at someone walking toward them. "Matty."

"Mom?" He gaped at the scene in front of him, standing frozen with a crisp twenty-dollar bill in his hand—which had no doubt come out of their joint checking and not the criminal's pocket. The guy probably had a sob story that pulled on Matt's heartstrings and made him decide to pay for the stolen meal.

Penny stood and took a step in his direction, then hesitantly said, "Matty, I'm so sorry. I—"

Matt engulfed Penny in a hug, blinking at Becky. When Penny hugged him tightly in return, tears filled his eyes. They stood like that for a full ten seconds until the waitress broke the emotional reunion up with a Styrofoam cup and a smile.

The two of them settled into the booth with Becky, slowly easing into a conversation that went on for half an hour. Occasionally, Matt or Penny would ask Becky a question or tell a story meant to include her, but she was just fine watching God's miracle unfold in front of her. She counted her blessings, the best of which was being Matthew Taylor's wife.

This man, who had been an unsung hero from the Horn of Africa to the headwaters of the French Broad River and many places in between, belonged to her. Their daughter would grow up being loved by a father who made a difference in the world, who saved people he would never know and forgave without hesitation. Nothing Becky had ever done or would ever do could top the accomplishment of making Matt fall in love with her . . . because she absolutely took full credit for that brilliant idea.

Author's Note

I was in the middle of writing a completely unrelated novel when the inspiration for my first Christmas novella hit me. The urge to write this story was so strong, I dropped everything and set to typing as fast as my fingers would move. I stayed awake more than one night, seeing the sunshine through my window before I stood from my computer. I remember posting a few lines the morning I finished the book. I'd written the entire thing in under a week. My amazing critique partners set to work right away, and the story was much improved and somewhat polished in a matter of a few days.

I hadn't even considered the possibility of publishing this year. It was too much too fast. But my developmental editor asked if I wanted to do it and told me she thought it was possible. My copyeditor agreed that there was no skin off her back. My cover designer worked her magic in record time. I remember thinking, "This is wild! Why am I doing it? I know I'll be stressed when it comes to formatting and proofreading and hitting publish."

Two weeks to the day of typing THE END, Hurricane Helene ripped through western North Carolina. Rosman went dark. Neighboring counties were literally swept away by one of the main characters of my story: the French Broad River.

At first, I didn't know what to do. Would it be insensitive or crass to publish the book in the aftermath of such disaster and loss? My critique partners—including one who lives in the hard-hit Ashe County—said it wouldn't be. Would people think I only wrote a story based in WNC to capitalize on the situation? Not likely, seeing as half of my books are based in Transylvania County already. I was uneasy about all of it but kept moving forward on schedule.

When I turned my focus to finding ways to help the people of Appalachia, it was a complete facepalm moment. I can picture God raising his eyebrow (definitely the left one) at how long it took for me to catch on. Of course, *this* was one of the roads God paved in advance. His hand was on it the entire way, from the inspiration and unrelenting motivation to every usual roadblock being mysteriously cast aside. It wasn't too much too fast. It was all I had to offer at the exact time of need.

This entire project stemmed from my love of the rural communities of the Blue Ridge Mountains. *Headwater Holiday* was always meant to be my gift to the people of Rosman—and not just the dedication and story, but the royalties. I pray the need for hurricane relief is short-lived. I look forward to the day profits from this story aren't necessary for anything more than football helmets or cans of paint for the senior rock (IYKYK). Regardless, this book belongs to you, Rosman. TIGER STRONG FOREVER!

All my love,

Hannah

About the Epigraph

Shortly after Hurricane Helene hit western North Carolina, a friend of mine penned this poem. Writing is so often therapeutic to us authors. **Jessica Whitmire's** words are the sort that bring healing to the reader as well. This is her heartrending love letter to the French Broad River:

As a little girl, I sailed your waters,
In a mighty green canoe.
I learned to swim, fish, and paddle,
On your shoals, it's where I grew.

My eyes have danced to your reflection,
As the sun mirrored off your skin.
From your banks, I've watched you glisten,
Sparking a light deep within.

As a woman, I have faced your weather,
I have watched you rise and fall.
Never did I fear a day
That you would take it all.

But you rose above your floodplain,
From your banks, you have escaped.

Horror and havoc, they're calling it,
And destruction was our fate.

As a mother, I came to you
To teach my son of life.
I want him to know your lines and drifts,
And how to mend and fight.

As a mother, I am sobbing
From what I've witnessed of your wrath.
Anger is what I'm feeling now,
You've broken my heart in half.

How do we go on from here?
What's left of you and I?
The future seems unreachable,
And I'm still asking you why.

As an Appalachian, I forgive you,
For without you, there is no us.
It's going to take some time, I know,
For you to regain my trust.

We can move forward together;
Together is where you've brought us all.
The love that's risen above the darkness
Has helped us all stand tall.

As a river, you are wise and wild,
So I hope you'll hear this prayer:
May God heal the land you've flowed through,
The people and the towns they're from.
May He ease your troubled spirit
And bring you calmness for many days to come.

Acknowledgements

To everyone who supported this project with your time, energy, money, and word of mouth: THANK YOU! It means the world to me and to all the people who will benefit from the profits of each book sold. Initially, the royalties will go toward rebuilding houses and riverbanks that were damaged and destroyed by Hurricane Helene. I hope you loved the story. Even if it wasn't your preferred genre, it was and will always be something special that you were a part of!

To my husband and kids—Thank you for supporting me and encouraging me, even when you'd rather have my undivided attention. I know that I'm blessed beyond measure to have a family who *gets* it.

To the Ballers: Carrie, Brianna, and Latisha—Thank you for making everything better with brainstorming, critiquing, and continually reminding me, "WE WRITE WHAT WE WANT!"

To Jennifer Q. Hunt—Thank you for finding that career-ending mistake I made with everyone's favorite Flynn. *chuckle* Also, thanks for giving me permission to (once again) break the mold!

To Heather Wood—Wow. The typos and overused italics. You'd think there would be less in a book half the size of my usual works. Whoops! Thank you for fixing all of the things!

To Kelsey Gietl—Thank you for the fast work and dealing with my wishy-washy antics. You deserve a medal!

To my beta readers: Myra, Christy, and Mahala—Thank you for reading this as soon as I sent it and getting notes back to me within hours. Y'all really boost the ego with that enthusiasm!

To the people of Rosman, NC—Thank you for being excited about my story and embracing this—the thing I have to offer. I hope I make y'all proud!

To my Jesus—As always, all praise, glory, and honor goes to the Savior of my soul and Giver of all life and inspiration.

About the author

HANNAH HOOD LUCERO is a wife, mom of three, Army veteran, and self-proclaimed word-slinger. While it is the brackish waters of the Mississippi Sound that flow through her veins, western North Carolina holds her heart. Her love for storytelling is the fruit of a lifetime of cultivation in the vibrant cultures of the Gulf Coast and the Blue Ridge Mountains. She currently resides in South Mississippi with her husband and three children on their ten-acre homestead. They have one dog, thirteen chickens, and at least fifty species of mosquitos, depending on the month of the year. When she isn't in the garden, at the stove, or homeschooling, she can be found at her computer—just follow the sound of frenetic typing. Her motto is, "Draft, edit, read, repeat."

Also by Hannah Hood Lucero

Young Adult
Cathey's Creek Road

The Sons of Vigilance Series
Already in the Kudzu
Beau on the Bayou
Crossfire at the Precipice
Dereliction of the Heart

Other Military Romantic Suspense
The Glory of Light

Find more details and all the latest news at hannahhoodlucero.com

Made in the USA
Columbia, SC
15 November 2024

46283204R00083